NICK'S MISSION

NICK'S MISSION

Claire Blatchford

 Lerner Publications Company ● Minneapolis

Library of Congress Cataloging-in-Publication Data

Blatchford, Claire H.
    Nick's mission / by Claire H. Blatchford.
        p.   cm.
    Summary: Nick, a deaf sixth grader, is upset about having to go to
speech therapy over the summer, until he and his dog stumble on some
dangerous smugglers and he learns the importance of being able to
communicate.
    ISBN 0-8225-0740-4
    [1. Deaf—Fiction. 2. Physically handicapped—Fiction.
3. Dogs—Fiction. 4. Mothers and sons—Fiction.] I. Title.
PZ7.B6139Ni   1995
[Fic]—dc20   95-856
                                                         CIP
                                                          AC

Manufactured in the United States of America
1 2 3 4 5 6 - BP - 99 98 97 96 95

For Edward

Nick slipped the hearing aid from his right ear, switched it off and dropped it in the kitchen drawer. He took a bagel from the refrigerator and hurried into the hallway to get his flippers, mask, and snorkel. All he wore was his bathing suit. His sixth grade had gotten out at noon for summer vacation and he was in a rush to get to the lake.

Wags, Nick's mutt, was already at the front door, waiting to go. Her stringy brown tail bounced back and forth like a windshield wiper. She went everywhere with him—she even swam with him in the lake. The only place she couldn't go was to school.

As Nick reached for the doorknob, his mother grabbed his arm. He looked up at her.

Her lips formed one word: "Therapy."

Nick shut his eyes. He did that when he didn't want to hear what people had to say. Therapy? On the day vacation began? How could they? It wasn't fair. Darn his mother and Mrs. Graves!

His mother patted his cheeks and ruffled his curly red-blond hair. He shook his head and refused to look at her.

When she tapped at his arm, Nick dropped the bagel and swung out at her blindly with the flippers. The mask and snorkel flew across the hall. No, he was *not* going to therapy.

Before he could escape, she'd bent him over, tripped him up and had pinned him to the floor. He couldn't even squirm. If only he was taller and heavier and didn't have such skinny arms and legs!

Nick's mother tickled him under the arms while Wags tried to lick his face. She tickled him until his sides ached and he opened his eyes.

"I'm . . . I'm gonna die," Nick gasped.

She stopped the tickling, pushed the dog away, and grinned at him. Like Nick she had blond hair but hers was golden blond and very straight. It was long, too, and was almost always clipped back at the nape of her neck.

"I'm sorry, Nick," she spoke very slowly as her blue eyes held his. "But you *have* to go to speech therapy. Come back to this world. Put your hearing aid back on."

Mrs. Graves always wore white blouses with tired, floppy bows at the throat. Her hair was brown, but she looked old enough to be Nick's grandmother. Maybe because her face was covered with pockmarks. The pockmarks made Nick think of the craters on the surface of the moon.

"She *looks* like a grave," Nick told his mother after his first session with the therapist.

His mother had laughed. Sometimes, when she picked up him and Wags at the front door of the clinic after therapy, she would say, "How was The Grave today?"

He'd make a face. Mrs. Graves made him say the dumbest things over and over, as if she didn't know what they meant:

"She sells seashells by the seashore."

"The king likes to sing and sing in the spring."

"Come, come, now, brown cow."

She would tell him to breathe through his teeth when he made his s's. She would hold his hand up in front of her mouth so he could feel her breath as she made her s. Then there were the l's. She would tell him to put his tongue on the roof of his mouth right behind his teeth whenever he made that sound. She made him look in the mirror as he did it. His tongue got *so* tired! Making *l*'s was harder than doing push-ups in gym.

Nick almost liked the lipreading sessions, though. Mrs. Graves usually read him the police log in the local paper. Nick was supposed to repeat everything he read on her lips. The names and addresses weren't always easy to pronounce, but the crimes stayed pretty much the same: speeding, jumping lights, making U-turns, trespassing. Every now and then something wild happened, like an accident or a robbery. In fact, that Monday, Mrs. Graves had read Nick a notice about a break-in at the local pet shop over the weekend. The cops listed it as vandalism. The animals had been let loose and pet food had been dumped all over the floor. Nick, who loved Firth's Pet Shop, had gone by after therapy to see if he could help clean up. To his disappointment, the store was closed and the lights were off. He hoped it was only temporarily closed.

"Happy vacation," Mrs. Graves said as Nick came into her office.

He shook his head.

"I thought you got out of school today."

"Yup, but I had to come here."

Mrs. Graves took both of his hands in hers. She did that when she had something important to say. Nick was tempted to shut his eyes but his mother was right behind him. He knew she would get mad if he did that.

"Nick, we're going to see a lot of each other this summer," Mrs. Graves said.

Nick's eyes nearly crossed.

"Mr. Stanton wants you to work with me every day." Mr. Stanton was the principal at Nick's school.

Every day? During the school year Nick had therapy only twice a week. How could they do that to him? He would go crazy with the cows and the seashells and the singing king. His tongue would get so tired it would fall off.

Nick pulled back, away from Mrs. Graves. Wags, who had settled in her customary spot by the door, cocked her head at him as if asking what was the matter.

Nick turned to his mother.

She gave a little nod. A nod that said, "I'm afraid so."

"What about Dad?" Nick parents were divorced. He and Wags usually went to visit his father in Maine for a month in the summer.

"You might see him for a week in August," she said, fingering one of the turquoise studs she always wore in her ears.

"But..."

"Nick, it's therapy or another school next year."

"Uhh... I'll go to another shool."

11

"No, Nick. You're *not* going away to a school for the deaf. And it's pronounced *sk . . . ool.*"

Mrs. Graves nodded in agreement. "Nick," she said, "you're smart. You *can* manage in public school. Mr. Stanton and all your teachers say you're a fantastic lip-reader. As a matter of fact, you're the best lip-reader I've ever seen—you'd make a good spy."

Nick almost grinned when she said that. He knew he was a pretty good lip-reader, even though he'd only been deaf since he'd had meningitis in first grade.

"He *is* a spy," Nick's mother put in. "He knows everything that's going on. He can read people the way you read the newspaper."

Nick frowned. His mother was being a bit *too* nice.

"Nick, " Mrs. Graves continued, "you're great at following things but the hearing aid doesn't really help you to hear yourself. Your speech is deteriorating—did you get that word?"

Nick nodded.

Nick's mother poked him with her elbow. She knew he was bluffing.

"De-tear-e-or-a-ting." Mrs. Graves drew the word out slowly. "What does it mean?"

Nick shrugged.

"It means your speech is getting worse. Some of your teachers say they can barely understand you. They say you talk too fast. Your words run together. Your classmates have trouble under-standing you, too. And we're all concerned be-cause you don't seem to have friends."

Nick shrugged again. He wished the grown-ups would get off his back about not having friends. He *did* have friends. He had Wags. (The tip of her tail gave a little twitch as he looked at her.) She was definitely his best friend. He didn't even have to open his mouth to talk with her. She understood everything. And he had his tropical fish, even though he couldn't exactly play with them the way he played with Wags. And there was Mrs. F., the owner of the pet shop, though she could be distant and opinionated at times. (He called her Mrs. F. because he had trouble pro-nouncing her name.) And there was the white pine out behind their apartment.

Nick had never talked with his mother about the pine, because his friendship with the tree didn't have anything to do with words. It had to do with feelings. When he sat up high in the branches of the pine, Nick felt as though he was with a wise, old friend—a friend who didn't fuss over his speech, or how he dressed, or how he did in classes. They'd just sit together peacefully, close to the open sky, enjoying the breezes while Wags waited down below. He felt free up in the pine, the way he felt free when he swam in the lake.

"Nick, we're talking about this world." His mother seemed to know what he was thinking.

13

"This world" was her term for the world of people. It meant school, church, therapy, family gatherings, and being friendly with neighbors even if you didn't feel friendly. It meant talking about problems like unemployment and the homeless. She had wanted him to join the Boy Scouts but he'd crossed his arms and shaken his head firmly. He *did* care about this world. He picked up trash when he went in the woods, and he was always taking turtles off the road—even big snappers that he had to grab by the tail—so they wouldn't be hit by cars. He'd never told her, but sometimes when he was up in the pine, he got this feeling in his chest. This feeling that he was going to do something big and important someday. Like figuring out how to get turtles and other animals to stay off the roads in the first place. Or saving the Great Barrier Reef when he became a deep-sea diver. In the meantime, he had no interest at all in wearing a uniform, visiting old people in nursing homes, singing campfire songs, and working for badges.

"You can't spend your whole life sitting in a tree, poking around in a pet shop, or snorkeling," she added.

Nick stuck out his tongue at her.

His mother did it back.

"Now, now," Mrs. Graves put both hands up. "It's just that we know your speech can be better, Nick. It's a matter of work and practice, that's all. Don't you want good speech?"

Nick shut his eyes. He'd had it! Good speech? Ugh! It sounded like good grades and being a good, sweet boy and all that crap. Deep-sea divers didn't spend their time worrying about getting good grades or shaking hands and saying, "Hello, Mrs. So-and-So, how are you today?" Deep-sea divers didn't waste time talking—they *did* things!

Nick expected his mother to poke him again with her elbow, but she didn't.

After a few minutes, he felt something wet and rough pass over his hand. He opened one eye and took a peek. Wags was sitting in front of him, grinning and wagging. Nick grinned back. She never let him stay angry or upset for long.

Nick opened his other eye and looked around. His mother was gone. She'd walked right out and left him with The Grave. Darn her!

Mrs. Graves sat in front of him reading the paper, waiting to start therapy.

Nick was so mad at his mother he stood up. "I . . . I want to go shwimmung."

Wags popped up, shook herself, and went to the door.

"*Sss*-wimm-*ing*," Mrs. Graves corrected him.

Nick ignored her.

"You plan to walk home?"

Nick nodded.

"That's a long walk. Your mother told me to tell you she'll drive you home after therapy if you'll meet her at the store." Nick's mother worked in a health food store about half a mile from the clinic.

"I don't want therapy." There—he'd said it!

For a second, Nick thought Mrs. Graves was going to cry. Her brown eyes looked watery. Was she sad about him? His speech wasn't worth crying about. Maybe he couldn't say the word *swimming* right but that wasn't going to keep him from swimming.

"I know you don't want therapy, Nick, but I know I can help you." Mrs. Graves paused. "Why don't we forget the speech work today and just do the lipreading?"

Nick sighed. Lipreading or no lipreading, he did not want therapy. All spring he'd been counting the days till vacation began. Counting the days till he could swim and snorkel from early morning till late afternoon with no interruptions. He *had* to swim and snorkel. He had to figure out how he was going to cross the lake alone and explore the waters on the other side. He even planned to keep a notebook of his explorations.

"I found a strange story in today's paper," Mrs. Graves continued. "I'll read it to you quickly. Then you can get a ride home with your mother. You'll get to the lake faster that way."

Nick sighed again and motioned for Wags to sit down. Mrs. Graves had better be quick!

2

"'A scarlet macaw was found dead in a North Chester cow pasture Tuesday afternoon'," Mrs. Graves read.

"Uh?" Nick interrupted her. "A *what?*"

"A scarlet macaw."

Although he really wanted to get going, Nick couldn't suppress his curiosity. "What's that?"

"It looks like a parrot of some kind." Mrs. Graves handed him the paper.

There on the front page was a photograph of a police officer holding a large, limp bird in both hands, the way an angler might hold a trout.

Nick drew in his breath quickly. What was a tropical bird like that doing in a cow pasture in Connecticut?

Mrs. Graves took the paper back before Nick could read the rest of the article himself.

" 'Dr. Winters, of the Northwoods Animal Shelter, examined the bird and said he thought it had died from exhaustion. No one knows where it came from. According to Dr. Winters, the scarlet macaw is one of the most popular South American parrots and is frequently pictured on the cover of travel brochures. It can measure up to twenty-eight inches and can weigh between two and three pounds. Unfortunately, the species is declining rapidly because of large-scale destruction of its forest habitat. It is no longer imported and can only be found in this country in zoos.' "

This was weird. *Very* weird.

"The only shoo in Connecticut is in Bridgeport," Nick said, more to himself than to Mrs. Graves. Bridgeport was about sixty miles away. Had the bird escaped from the zoo?

"Zzz-ooo," Mrs. Graves corrected him.

Then, instead of asking Nick to tell her the details of the article the way she usually did, Mrs. Graves ripped the front page off the paper and handed it to him. "I thought you'd be interested. Want to keep it?"

Nick took the paper and looked, again, at the photo. The limp bird made him feel slightly sick to his stomach. It was the same feeling he got when he saw dead animals on the road.

"Let's talk about it tomorrow," Mrs. Graves said. "You can go swimming now."

Nick blinked. She *had* been quick. She was letting him go. At first he was too surprised to move. Then he stuffed the article in his shorts pocket, nodded good-bye, and hurried out of the office and down the hall to the front door, Wags at his heels.

Firth's Pet Shop was seven stores down from the health food store. Nick's steps quickened as the door of the pet shop came into view. The lights were on and the yellow sign with OPEN in big blue letters was up. He gestured for Wags to wait for him outside and went in.

Nick saw in a glance that the aquariums were okay. Sometimes, on weekends in the winter, he helped Mrs. F. clean out the filters, replace the lights, or transfer fish and snails to new bowls.

He found Mrs. F. in the back aviary, scratching the head of one of the baby cockatiels. White cockatiels were her specialty. Nick thought she looked a bit like one herself, with her gray-white hair piled in a loose bun on top of her head, and her big, curved nose.

Nick tapped on the window.

Mrs. F. gave him a curt nod.

Nick knew she couldn't be hurried. She would come out when she was through talking with her birds. He circled around the store, relief welling up in him as he went. He saw the ferrets, rabbits, and hamsters in their cages. The puppies napped. One of the snakes was missing, but he knew it wasn't poisonous. Apart from that, things looked okay.

"It was NOT vandalism," Mrs. F. said a few minutes later, without even a "hello" to Nick. "They're crooks. The cops won't listen to me just because the cash register and the safe weren't touched and the puppies weren't taken." Nick knew that a purebred spaniel could fetch up to $500.

"Did they take anything?"

"Birdseed."

Nick almost laughed. Who would want to steal birdseed?

"And vitamins," Mrs. F. added. "Six bottles. I keep track of EVERYTHING here."

"But why?"

She threw up her hands. "Heaven knows!"

"You aren't going to close down, are you, Mrs. F.?"

"Close down? NEVER! Why would I do that?" She glared at him.

Nick gave a little shrug and kept quiet. Mrs. F. got angry easily. Nick's mother said Mrs. F. would have more business if she weren't so touchy, but Nick understood the things that upset her. What animal *wanted* to be poked at by little kids? And how were birds supposed to know that gum dropped in their cages would stick to their beaks?

"Don't you know by now that I'm not in this for the money?" Mrs. F. asked.

Nick gave one quick little nod, though he wasn't sure what she meant.

"There has to be *someone* to show people how to look after pets," Mrs. F. continued. "Most pet stores don't care if the fish die a month after you buy them. I care. I expect my customers to care. You can't buy a pet the way you buy a can of soda. You don't just toss out the money, get what you want out of it, and then discard it."

Nick put a hand over his mouth to hide his grin. She reminded him of his mother when she got going about health food. And how his mother hated soda!

Mrs. F. went to answer the telephone. Eager to get home and then to the lake, Nick waved good-bye.

Mrs. F. gave him another curt nod from behind the counter.

Nick and Wags walked down the sidewalk, Nick still grinning. The pet shop was okay after all.

His grin disappeared fast, though, when he saw the blue-and-white pickup truck parked outside the health food store. The truck belonged to Carlos. Carlos was the new gardener at the convent across the lake from the public beach. He had a bushy mustache that almost completely covered his mouth, making it impossible for Nick to see his lips. Carlos also had bushy eyebrows that

21

went up and down all the time, and dark eyes that darted about.

Drat! Nick's mother would probably want him to help carry in the vegetables. (Carlos sold his organic vegetables at the store.) Then she would probably want to talk with Carlos for "a little while." They never talked for "a little while." They always went on and on and on. It had happened twice, and Nick hated it. He wished he had gone straight home.

Sure enough, Nick's mother gestured for him when he came in.

"Get the peas in Carlos's truck, Nick."

Nick gritted his teeth and went back out. She hadn't even said please.

Nick deliberately did not look at Carlos as he put the bags of peas on the counter. He went back out with Wags to his mom's station wagon, climbed in, dug the newspaper article out of his pocket, and reread it. He should have shown it to Mrs. F. He'd show it to her the next time he went by the pet shop. She would have ideas about where the bird had come from.

"Nicholas Wilder," Nick's mother said when she finally came out to the car to take him home, "you've been rude to two people today."

Nick shoved the article back in his pocket and glared at her. "Suzanne Pierce," he wanted to say,

using her full name, "don't lecture me!" But he
didn't. That would really make her mad. Darn
her! Couldn't she see how badly he wanted to go
swimming? Couldn't she remember that vacation
had started this afternoon?

"You were rude to Mrs. Graves and you were
rude to Carlos."

"I don't like him." Nick hadn't meant to say
that; the words just popped out.

Her eyes challenged him. "Why not?"

"He's too nervous. His eyes jump all over."

"Of course he's nervous! How would you feel if
you were in a strange country, could barely speak
the language, and knew people thought you were
stupid because of that?"

Nick's mouth fell open. "He doesn't know
English?"

She shook her head. "Not very well. He's from
Mexico. I speak Spanish with him. I thought I told
you that."

Nick stared at his mother. Had she told him?
His face got warm. He couldn't remember. Sometimes, when he was tired from watching faces, he
"switched off" and didn't bother to get every
word his mother said. This usually happened
when she talked about other people. Seemed to
him she took care of an awful lot of people. There
was a lady in a wheelchair whom she went to see
every Monday afternoon. And there was Mr.
Zetterberg, the barber, whose wife had died at

Christmas. Nick's mom delivered meals-on-wheels, too. As for her speaking Spanish, he was amazed. He hadn't known until then that she could speak another language.

"Why's he here?" Nick asked.

"He was in California for a month before he came to the convent. He's in this country to earn money for his family. They're very poor."

"You mean his family's at the convent?"

She shook her head. "They're in southern Mexico. He sends money to them. He has five children and two grandchildren to support."

"When's he going back?"

"He doesn't know. It's pretty lonely for him here, Nick. Whenever he comes to the store I try to help him with his English."

So that was why they talked so much. Nick made a face. Why did his mother have to help him? Maybe she knew Spanish, but she wasn't a teacher, or a social worker, or a therapist. "Can't he go to Mrs. Graves?"

"Mrs. Graves isn't a language teacher. There's someone in New Haven but that's a long way for him to go." She paused. "I *want* to help him, Nick. Are you jealous or something?"

Nick punched her lightly. Jealous? Why would he be jealous?

She grinned and punched him back.

"I'd appreciate it if you'd apologize to Mrs. Graves tomorrow," she said. "She really wants to help you."

Nick shrugged.

"Nick, I think you're making a mountain out of a molehill. Therapy won't be bad. It'll only be an hour and a half every morning. You'll be able to swim every afternoon and all weekend. You might even get sick of swimming."

Nick shook his head. She didn't understand how important the snorkeling was to him. It wasn't just that he wanted to watch the fish, he wanted to see what life was like in the lake. Was the water clear everywhere? Were the fish okay? Were there too many water lilies and reeds? (He'd read in science class that that can be a bad sign. It can mean fertilizer used on the land is running off into the lake.) If she knew he planned to explore the lake she might worry about him and tell Amy, the lifeguard at the public beach, to keep an eye on him. He certainly didn't want that. If he told his mom he felt he had to check out the lake, she would probably say he was imagining things. Wasn't she always saying the Wilders had weird, wild imaginations?

"I think we might be able to speed things up, " Nick's mother went on. "Mrs. Graves gave me a book of sentences and words we can work on together at home."

Nick frowned. "You mean homework?"

"Sort of."

Nick kicked the dashboard. Homework? Homework in the summer?

He folded his arms over his chest, turned away from her, and stared out the passenger window. Shutting his eyes wasn't going to do much good. HOW was he going to get out of therapy?

3

What if he ran away? What if he headed straight for the other side of the lake that very afternoon and camped out under one of the willows? Nick's heart sped up.

He rolled his window down and leaned out as if to see the way ahead better. There were two huge old willows on the shore opposite the public beach, about a quarter mile away. They grew out over the water. During the winter Nick had seen deer by the trees, drinking from the lake. In the spring he'd seen swans, ducks, and geese coming and going from under the curtain of yellow-green willow leaves. Nick would be hidden by the leaves. His mother would never know where he'd gone. He could take his sleeping bag, water bottle, and backpack full of dry meal for Wags (even if she wasn't wild about it), and granola, carrots, and apples for himself.

There were two big questions, though. First, would he get into trouble if he was caught camping over there? (There were NO TRESPASSING signs everywhere on the opposite shore.) Second, exactly how would he get there?

The land on which the willows grew belonged to the convent where Carlos worked. The nuns were cloistered. Nick's mother had explained to him that "cloistered" meant they never went into town or anywhere, and rarely saw anyone outside of the convent. She told him they wore long gray gowns and always covered their hair. Sounded weird to Nick. He wondered what the nuns did all day and what happened if they got sick and had to go to a doctor.

The dark roof of the main convent building was barely visible from the public beach. The big house had been a grand estate forty years earlier. Nick's mother had once shown him old photos of it in the library. There had been a dock, rose gardens, pebbled paths, fountains, and a lawn leading down from the main house to the willows at the water's edge. Now brambles, shrubs, and vines had taken over. The boathouse was still there but it was shabby, shuttered, and mostly hidden by a tall brownish thicket. Nick couldn't believe the nuns ever went down by the lake. It was too overgrown. They'd probably never know he was there. He'd be so quiet, so invisible, he'd be like one of the wild animals.

How Nick would get there was the big question. Kids under fifteen weren't allowed to swim across the lake alone and Amy, the lifeguard, knew that he was twelve. He'd have to go when Amy wasn't around. But even if he did swim across, how would he transport his food and gear? Walking around the lake was out of the question. It would take forever; there were too many fences and swampy spots. As for coming in the back way, there was only one road and it led to the convent, nowhere near the lake.

Nick scowled and bit his lip. He didn't see how he could pull it off. Maybe he should forget about the lake and run away to Maine. But if he did that he'd have to talk to people to get there, and they might not understand him. They might think he was retarded or something. There was also the matter of money. He wouldn't be able to get very far without money unless he dipped into his wet-suit fund. He had $70 in the fund—$20 of allowance money he'd saved and the $50 his grandparents had given him for Christmas. Those $70 had him exactly halfway to the wet suit he'd picked out. His mother would want to know what he was up to if he asked her to take some of it out of the bank. And why spend it on a bus ticket?

Nick felt a familiar tapping at his arm as they stopped for a traffic light.

He turned to look at his mother.

"You trying to get away from me?"

Nick shook his head and turned back to the passenger window. Darn! Not only was she stronger than he was, she could practically read his mind. It wasn't fair! How could he ever get his own way? Maybe if he locked himself in his room and refused to come out, she would get worried and would back down on therapy.

Nick knew that idea wouldn't work either. His mother was too smart. She would probably climb in the window to argue with him (their apartment was on the ground floor), or she'd set a trap for him right outside his window or his door. Worse yet, she might hide his snorkeling equipment.

At the moment the car pulled up beside their apartment, Nick hit upon the perfect plan. It was so simple he couldn't believe it at first. He just wouldn't talk.

Not talking would be a lot easier than shutting his eyes or locking himself in his room. That was it! He wouldn't open his mouth except to eat or drink. Mrs. Graves could squeeze his hands until they were sticky as jam but she wouldn't get a word out of him. His mother could try to have one of her eye-to-eye, heart-to-heart talks. He would outstare her. He wouldn't talk if she tickled him. He might scream, but he wouldn't talk. When she realized he meant business and there was no point in his going to therapy, she would back down and leave him alone.

"I'll be at the store," Nick's mother said, grabbing his arm before he could get out. "You going swimming?"

He nodded.

She ruffled his hair. "I know therapy is a pain, Nick. But, later on, you'll be glad you did it."

Nick drew back. He didn't want to listen. He wanted to be on his way.

"Okay, okay!" She gave him a push. "Go on and get busy collecting more freckles. I'll be home by 5:30."

A few minutes later, Nick dropped his hearing aid in the kitchen drawer, let Wags out the back door, and stuffed his snorkeling equipment in the metal basket on the back of his bike.

The public beach had no dock. Boats couldn't be moored on the lake. Only portable sailboats, canoes, dinghies, and Windsurfers were allowed. There was a parking lot, a grassy area with picnic tables, the sandy swimming area, and the chunky wooden raft anchored about fifty feet from the beach. The beach had opened four days before, but no one was swimming because the weather was more like May than June. A bunch of little kids dug in the sand while their mothers talked. Amy was curled up in the tall white chair in her green sweatpants and sweatshirt. She jerked her head at Nick to acknowledge his presence before returning to her paperback. When she didn't have to watch the lake carefully, she read.

Nick stepped into the water. It was freezing. He'd been taking cold showers all spring to build up his tolerance for cold water, but the goose pimples popped out on his arms and legs anyway. Wags waded in beside him and lapped at the water.

Nick knew he'd chicken out if he just stood there. He put his flippers, mask, and snorkel on and plunged in quickly. The coldness knocked the breath right out of him. For a second he was too surprised to move. Then, without a backward glance, he flipped out hard and fast in the direction of the raft, Wags paddling along behind.

Further out, Nick took his first look down. Another shiver ran through him. The water was gray-green but absolutely clear, still, and quiet. So quiet. No lips to read, no faces to watch, no sounds. He could see the rocks at the bottom and strands of duckweed here and there. Silver fish with blue markings darted this way and that before his hands.

A tiny turtle on the raft, with orange bands on its black neck, blinked as Nick looked up and took hold of the ladder. They stared at each other. Then the turtle's legs shot out, and it pushed its way to the end of the board, plopped headfirst into the lake, and swam away. Nick laughed. He made a couple of circles on his back around the raft. Wags followed, her head bobbing up and down, her tail wiggling like a snake behind her. Nick glanced from her to the shore. Amy read her book, the mothers talked to each other, and the little kids played in the sand. No one paid any attention to them. He felt warm and happy.

Then he saw a man at the end of the beach, standing right near the grass. He wore shiny silver sunglasses, a jacket, a necktie, and dark pants. He had a pair of binoculars in one hand and was looking toward the raft. As Nick stared at him, he raised a hand and waved.

Nick stared.

The man waved again.

Nick ducked behind the raft.

Was the guy waving at him? He took another look.

The man waved for the third time.

Nick's heart sped up. His mother had told him many times to beware of strangers. "Don't even try to read their lips," she'd warned him. "Just get away from them."

He wished he had an oxygen tank and could sink down underwater and disappear from sight.

Nick waited for a while behind the raft with

Wags. He took another peek. The man was still there, still watching. Nick's teeth began to chatter, just a little at first and then harder. He felt as though he was in one of the big rectangular freezers in the supermarket. If he didn't get moving soon his body temperature was going to get dangerously low.

Nick decided to swim to the other end of the beach, away from the man. He pushed off from the raft and flipped fast, head down, snorkel up. There wasn't time to look around or listen to the stillness. The fish shot away from him like silver arrows, in all directions. He didn't dare look up until he saw the sand.

Nick almost swallowed a mouthful of water. The man was walking down the beach toward him, half of his red necktie flapping back over his shoulder. He was tall—taller than Nick's father, very thin, and had longish brown hair. His silver sunglasses reflected the sun. Nick hated sunglasses, especially shiny sunglasses. It was almost impossible to read people's lips when he couldn't see the expressions in their eyes. The eyes told him if people were looking at him and talking to him. They told him if people were friendly or hostile, truthful or fake. When he couldn't see their eyes, he felt like he was talking to a blank wall.

Nick was pretty sure the man was looking at him. Then the man's mouth started moving.

Nick did as his mother had told him—he didn't

even try to read the man's lips. He kicked his flippers off, clutched them to his chest, and sprinted
up the beach with the mask and snorkel still on.
Amy glanced up briefly, gave Nick a good-bye
nod, and went on reading.

No one stopped Nick as he jammed his stuff
into the basket and fumbled with the bike lock.
He took one quick backward glance to make sure
Wags was coming and almost dropped his bike.
Wags was wagging her stringy, wet tail at the man.

Nick stared. Wags was hardly ever friendly
with strangers. What was going on? Was the guy
offering her something sweet to eat? Wags had a
real sweet tooth. She loved cookies, cake, and
candy. She could peel wrappers off candy bars
and would dig through mountains of trash for
bits of cookies in discarded boxes. Sweets were
the only way a stranger could get close to her.
Close enough to touch her—or catch her.

Nick gave two quick, loud, urgent claps to tell
Wags he was leaving. Her ears went up. He gave
two more claps to let her know he meant business.

She started toward him.

Nick hopped on his bike and pedaled furiously
down the road.

Wags followed. Nick didn't look back once.

4

Nick locked the front and back doors when he got home. He took the cover off his TTY. There was the typewriter keyboard with the narrow rectangular screen above it. Above the screen, where the typed words appeared, were two rubber suction cups. He placed the telephone receiver facedown on the suction cups.

Since the words that are typed on one TTY can only be transcribed by another phone on a TTY, Nick's mother had a machine at the health food store just for talking with him. But before Nick could dial her number, he remembered his no-talk, no-therapy plan. If he called her and told her about the man at the beach, she might come home and ask him all kinds of questions. Then he'd have to talk. Maybe his imagination *was* running wild. Maybe the stranger just wanted to know where Nick had gotten his snorkeling stuff or something like that.

Nick took the phone off the TTY and put it back on the hook. His father also had a TTY in his cabin in Maine. Nick knew he'd be at the lumberyard where he worked. Besides, if Nick could reach him, his father would probably call his mother. Or the police. No, Nick decided, he wasn't going to talk. He was going to stick with his plan and hope that the tall guy with the sunglasses and red necktie wasn't at the beach the next day.

Wags hurried into the bedroom as Nick finished dressing. She poked at Nick's leg with her nose and raced back into the hall. That was her way of telling Nick someone was ringing the doorbell.

With a beating heart, Nick peered out from behind the living room curtains. He let out a sigh of relief. It was Aaron Klein. Aaron was a year younger than Nick and had moved into the house across the street the previous summer. They hadn't seen much of each other during the winter because Aaron attended a private school.

Nick opened the front door halfway.

Aaron stood there like a little round brown mouse huddled in the corner of a cage. Nick could almost imagine Aaron with a tail tucked tight against his legs.

Aaron held something out for Nick. It was Nick's striped beach towel. "You dropped it on the sidewalk."

Nick took the towel with a nod of thanks. He hadn't even noticed it was missing. How could he have been so careless? If the man had been following him, he would've seen it and figured out where Nick lived.

"You . . . you want to try Tetris?" Aaron asked before Nick could say good-bye.

Nick screwed up his face as though thinking the matter over. He didn't want to admit he didn't know what Aaron was talking about or if he'd even read his lips properly.

"Daddy fixed my computer," Aaron added.

Nick scratched his head. He hadn't known Aaron's computer was broken and couldn't have cared less. Mr. Klein was a computer sales rep and instructor. Aaron could sound like a computer teacher, too. The one time Nick had gone over to the Klein's house he'd gotten a horrible headache from trying to understand all the weird computer terms—genies, modems, CD-ROM, viruses, and all that. It was like another language, a language Nick wasn't interested in learning. What really bothered Nick about Aaron, though, was that Aaron was such a wimp. He wouldn't swim out to the raft at the lake, he wouldn't try the mask and snorkel, and he was afraid to touch a turtle.

"Then Daddy got me Tetris," Aaron continued. "It's fun."

"I've . . . I've got to go," Nick stammered. "Bye."

He saw the disappointment in Aaron's eyes as he shut the door. What did Aaron expect? Was he going to hang around Nick's house all summer begging him to play computer games? Why couldn't the kid grow up and stop calling his father "Daddy"?

Nick fed Wags. Then he fed his tropical fish. Then he got his notebook and started his first entry for the season:

June 16: Got out for vacation.

Nick stopped. The day certainly hadn't gone as he'd expected with the news about therapy and the possibility of his attending another school. A new school? A school for deaf kids? The thought gave him a hollow feeling in his stomach. He'd never met another deaf kid in his life. He shrugged and pushed the thought out of his mind. September seemed as far away as China right then. He went on with his notebook entry:

June 16: Got out for vacation.
Swam to raft. Saw painted turtle,
seaweed, minnows, sunfish (I think—must check this). REAL cold!

Nick put the notebook back under his pillow and went into the living room. He switched the TV on. There weren't any nature programs. The only show with closed captioning subtitles was full of those people who talked too much. Nick pulled out his favorite *National Geographic* video and settled down on the sofa with Wags at his feet for an hour and a half of underwater adventures.

Wags started wagging and squirming at the front door before the film ended. That meant Nick's mother was home. She had an enormous box in her arms. She carried it into the house and put it down in the middle of the living room.

"For you," she told Nick. "Happy vacation."

He got a knife from the kitchen and slit the box open. Inside was an inflatable orange rubber raft and two plastic oars. He pulled everything out eagerly. There was a large life preserver, too. Nick couldn't stop grinning. Now he knew how he was going to get across the lake. He would be able to take his camping gear over and camp out after all. He'd do that if the no-talk plan fell through. He threw his arms around his mother and hugged her.

"We'll take it to the gas station after supper and pump it up," she said. "Want spaghetti?"

Nick nodded. He loved spaghetti, even green spinach spaghetti from the health food store.

"Was the lake cold?"

He nodded again and grinned some more. The rubber raft made him want to grin.

"I bet you're the first person in town to go swimming this year."

He gave a small, pleased shrug.

Her blue eyes held his firmly. "You want to practice the sentences now? Or later, before going to bed?"

Nick punched the air with both fists. So, she was trying to make up for the therapy by buying him a raft! The nerve! He shook his head.

She put both hands up. "Okay, I get the message. We won't do them now. I'll start supper."

She went out to the kitchen.

Nick kicked the sofa. He couldn't stay angry for long, though. Not with the raft. He unfolded it. He was sure, even though it was deflated and looked more like a collapsed tent than a boat, that it was going to be just the right size for him and Wags. He piled all the sofa pillows inside it and coaxed Wags onto it before flopping down beside her to watch the rest of the video.

"The snow peas are from Carlos," Nick's mother said as she passed the salad bowl to Nick at supper.

Nick pushed the snow peas to one side of the bowl and took most of the peppers and carrots.

41

He didn't want to have to think about Carlos.

"I'm worried about him," Nick's mother continued. "He pulled one of his teeth out. That's why I got mad at you for being rude. Did you see how swollen his face was?"

Nick shook his head and his eyes got big. Carlos had pulled his own tooth out? With what? A pliers? That would be something. Nick wanted to ask how Carlos had done it but he kept quiet.

"He said it was hurting too much," she continued. "He's never been to a dentist in his life, can you imagine that?"

Nick shook his head.

"I gave him a bottle of zinc tablets. If he's not better when he brings the vegetables Monday, I'm going to take him to Dr. Woocher."

Nick went on eating.

"He's probably tough as an ox, though." Nick's mother stopped, her hand resting on the barrette that held her hair back. "Hey, I've got an idea."

Nick cocked his head. He hoped her idea had nothing to do with Carlos.

"Why don't we invite Aaron to come along when we go to pump up the raft? We can get yogurt cones afterwards."

Nick gave one quick shake of his head.

"I was thinking of it for him, not for you, Nick. It would do him good to get out. His mother worries about him."

Nick rolled his eyes. Here she was, playing

counselor again. He also had the vague suspicion that she might have talked behind his back with Aaron's mother about *him*. He could hear her worrying aloud about his social life. Couldn't she stay out of his affairs? Couldn't she see he didn't want anything to do with the wimp?

Nick's mother brought her fist down on the table. She did it so hard Nick nearly jumped out of his chair.

"For heaven's sakes, say something!"

Nick shrugged, looked down, and suppressed a grin. Now the battle was going to begin.

She banged on the table again to get his attention. "Want to be tickled?"

He glared at her.

"Are you a monkey or a cat?"

He ignored the question. If she tickled him again he was going to bite.

"Oh, come on Nicky! You're being rude to *me* now. What's the matter? Tell me!"

He swallowed. Her blue eyes were really begging him to talk.

They stared at each other for one long moment.

Nick was close, very close, to yelling, "I HATE THERAPY! IT STINKS! I WON'T GO TO THERAPY!" but she got up and walked away before the words could come out. She went to the counter and picked up the phone—Nick couldn't hear it ringing—and spoke into it.

Nick stood up. The phone was always barging

in and taking her away when he had something to say. Always. He hated the thing! Okay, that settled it, he was not going to talk, no matter how upset she got. He might even give up talking for good.

He started for the back door.

But wait—his mother was waving at him. She had put the phone on the TTY. That meant all she heard on the phone was the clicking of TTY typewriter keys. The call was for *him*. Oh great! Probably his father. He would tell his father all about the homework and the crazy, insane plans for him to have therapy every day.

"Dad." The word appeared on Nick's TTY screen as he typed. "I'm here. GA." GA was the signal for the other person to talk. It meant, "Go Ahead."

"Is this Nick Wilder speaking? GA."

"Yes Dad. GA."

"This is the Connecticut Relay Operator with a call for you from the Four Seasons Sports Store. Can you come in tomorrow morning at 10:00? GA."

Nick scratched his head. It wasn't his father calling. He knew the relay operator was a telephone operator who relayed messages from people without TTYs to people with TTYs. He had used the operator a couple of times to call Mrs. Graves, but never the sports store. Why would the sports store people want to see him?

He looked for his mother. She'd left the kitchen.

"Why? GA."

"Peter wants to talk with you. Can you be there? GA."

Peter? Who was Peter? Nick knew the faces of the people who worked at the sports store, but not their names. His mother would know their names but he wasn't about to ask her. Was Peter the salesperson Nick and his mother had bought the snorkeling equipment from? Or was Peter the guy at the cash register?

Nick scratched his head again. He didn't know what to do. Maybe they'd made some mistake and were calling the wrong person.

Then Nick remembered something. When Nick was getting his bathing suit a few weeks earlier, the clerk at the cash register had shown Nick a photo of himself in a scuba diving outfit. The clerk had told Nick's mother he would take Nick along the next time he went scuba diving, to show him what it was like. Of course, that was it! Peter was the one at the cash register. He'd taken their phone number and the number of the relay operator. He had to be the one.

Nick was so excited he couldn't type properly. "ppk ... I mean ... ok. ... GA," he replied.

"OK, Nick. Peter says he will see you at 10:00 tomorrow at the Four Seasons Sports Store. GA or to SK." SK meant Stop Keying, or good-bye.

"SK," typed Nick.

Nick's mother came back in the kitchen as he

switched off the TTY.

"That was a short call," she said. "So you're not talking to your father either?"

Nick shrugged and put a hand over his mouth to keep from smiling. It was the first time he'd received a call on the TTY all for himself from someone other than his mother or father. He could see his mother was curious, very curious. She didn't know who had called. She didn't know he was going to the sports store at 10:00 the next day. He liked having a secret all his own. Wouldn't she be surprised when she learned he was going scuba diving?

"You're a stubborn one," she said wagging a finger at him. "You're not going to talk?"

He shook his head.

"How come?"

He shrugged.

She took a step toward him but Nick was too quick. He slipped around the kitchen table away from her.

"Nick, really, we need to talk!"

He didn't respond.

"Is it because of therapy?"

He nodded.

"You mean you're not going to talk because of therapy?"

He nodded again.

She rubbed her chin and thought a while.

"Well, then," she finally said, "I won't talk to

you until you talk to me."

Nick couldn't keep from grinning.

His mother grinned back.

He put out his hand and she slapped it. They had a deal.

After the dinner dishes were done Nick and his mother put the rubber raft in the car. Wags joined them in the front seat. They took the raft to the gas station and pumped it up. It just barely fit in the back of the station wagon.

Then they bought big, soft yogurt cones. Nick had to eat what his mother got him, which was boring old vanilla, because he couldn't say what he wanted. He didn't care though. It was nice, for a change, not having to talk, or to listen to his mother talking. She really could get going sometimes. Nick gave Wags the bottom half of his cone. She ate it in one gulp, licked her chops, and wiggled all over.

Back at home, Nick climbed up high into the pine tree. He was so psyched about the scuba diving, he had to hold onto the tree trunk. Maybe Peter would let him try the scuba equipment sometime in the lake. Nick would be able to go underwater. He would really be able to look at the fish. He would be able to swim across the lake without anyone knowing where he was. That would be neat. It would be even better than rowing across in the rubber raft. Maybe Peter would take him to the Sound or to Cape Cod or Block Island sometime, to try diving there. He couldn't stop imagining all the wonderful possibilities.

5

Nick woke the next morning at 9:00. Except for the time he'd been sick, he'd never slept so late in his life. He leapt out of bed and hurried into the kitchen. One place, his own, was set at the table. On one side of his cereal bowl was the speech book, on the other side was a note.

Catface,
    If you've discovered it's impossible to get through life without talking, please ride your bike to the clinic for therapy at 10 A.M. If you haven't made this discov-

ery, please call Mrs. Graves on your TTY and let her know you aren't coming. We don't want to waste her time. I'll be home before 12 to take the raft to the lake.

Love,
Mum Catface

Delighted, Nick crumpled the note into a ball and threw it at Wags. She caught it in midair and raced into the living room, Nick close behind. She wouldn't let him catch her. They did a couple of wild circles around the apartment before Nick collapsed on the sofa. He knew he would have to talk to his mother at some point, but right then he was too excited about getting out of therapy and the meeting with Peter to think about much else.

Wags dropped the paper ball in front of Nick and wagged expectantly. He threw the ball again, then again while wolfing down a bowlful of granola. Soon the note was in shreds.

Nick got dressed, locked up the apartment, and started off to town on his bike with Wags following.

Halfway to the Four Seasons Sports Shop, Nick slowed down and then came to a stop at the side of the road. How was he going to talk with Peter? He'd never talked with the people at the sports shop. His mother had always done the talking. Would he be able to read Peter's lips? Even if Mrs.

Graves had said he was the best lip-reader she'd ever had, Nick knew there were times when he had trouble. Mumblers, people who didn't look at him, people who moved around when they were talking or talked too fast, and men with mustaches like Carlos, were hard, if not impossible, to lip-read. At least the two guys who worked at the store didn't have hair all over their faces.

Nick frowned. Wags cocked her head at him. Nick wanted to be sure he understood *everything* Peter said. He couldn't afford to miss anything. He dug around in his pockets. There was the article about the scarlet macaw. He also found a pencil stub and a paper bag with a few peanuts from the health food store. He tossed a couple of the nuts to Wags and popped the rest in his mouth. He would ask Peter to write down all the information about where they were going, to be sure he got it right.

There was still the matter, however, of his talking to Peter. Was he going to talk, nod, gesture, write notes, or what? If he did talk and his mother found out, she would throw a fit. She would call him a sneaky coward for refusing to speak to her or Mrs. Graves and then talking behind their backs. There was also the possibility that Peter might have trouble understanding him. That settled it in Nick's mind. He *wasn't* going to talk.

When Nick got to the sports store, he nodded at Wags to tell her to stay by his bike. He ran a hand through his hair before strolling in casually through the open door.

The man at the cash register was talking to a customer and didn't look Nick's way. It was exactly 10:00.

Nick looked at the goggles, masks, and flippers. Each time he took a look, he looked beyond the merchandise to the man at the cash register. The guy was a real talker! He was so busy talking he hadn't even noticed Nick had come in. Nick's throat began to feel dry.

At ten past 10:00, Nick approached the cash register. The man looked down at him. "Hi, Nick. What's up?"

Nick's face began to burn. The guy obviously wasn't waiting for him.

Nick smoothed the bag out on the top of the counter and wrote, "Where is Peter?" He wished he knew Peter's last name. Before he could show the message to the guy behind the counter, he felt a hand on his shoulder. He looked up.

Another man had appeared out of nowhere. He had broad shoulders and stood very straight. He was dressed in a green shirt and brown pants. There was a little smile on his lips and another smile in his greenish brown eyes.

"Nick Wilder?" the stranger asked.

Nick nodded.

"I'm Peter. I called you last night." He was easy to understand. He didn't speak too fast, or too slowly, and he looked directly at Nick.

Nick stared back. He liked the straightforward look in the man's eyes. It made him feel he was being talked to as a person, not as a kid.

"You're deaf?" The man gestured at Nick's ears.

Nick gave a quick, curt nod.

"You sign?" His hands made circles in the air as he spoke.

So he was using sign language. Nick shook his head. He'd seen sign language on TV but he didn't know any. His mother wasn't too keen on his learning it. She thought it was more important for him to work on his speech. She said more people spoke with their voices than with their hands.

"I'm surprised you don't sign. I'd be glad to teach you some signs if you want."

Nick couldn't respond. He was too confused. He could understand everything the man said, but where had he come from? Who was he? What did he want? What about the scuba diving?

"I got your name and phone number here yesterday," the man explained. "I asked them if they knew of a boy with snorkeling equipment and a dog that liked to swim. They knew whom I was talking about right away."

Some customers had come to the cash register. The man drew Nick over by the fishing rods where they would be out of the way.

"Do you remember me?"

Nick frowned. There was something familiar

about him. What was it?

Peter was tall, a good deal taller than Nick's father, and he had longish brown hair. And then it hit him. Nick's heart jumped. It was the guy from the beach. Only the shiny silver sunglasses, the dark jacket, red necktie, and binoculars were missing. What a slowpoke he was! Why hadn't he realized that right away? Before he could turn for the door, Peter's hand was on his arm.

"Don't go, Nick, I won't hurt you." His eyes were sincere. They were also friendly.

Nick stood there, frozen.

"I saw you swimming yesterday. You're a fine swimmer. I saw the way you flipped all over, as if you were part fish."

Nick relaxed a bit. Part fish? He liked that.

"You're brave . . . . I wouldn't go in that water if you paid me."

Nick gave a little shrug.

"Doesn't the cold bother you?"

Nick shook his head.

"Then you are part fish," said Peter with a grin.

Nick tried not to smile but it wasn't easy. Peter's friendly smile made him want to smile back. He still wasn't sure he could trust this stranger. What did he want?

"Well, Nick, it's like this. I want to know if you can help me."

Nick cocked his head.

"I wondered if you could do some swimming

for me since *I'm* not part fish."

Nick's heart gave a jump. Had Peter lost something valuable in the lake? A credit card? A ring? A gold bracelet? Sure, he was ready to dive for it, whatever it was.

"Can't you talk at all?" Peter asked, still signing. His eyes were concerned.

Nick shook his head. He liked not talking. It made things easier. He didn't have to explain everything. All he had to do was to nod or shake his head when people asked him questions. Not talking made him feel mysterious and powerful.

"You say you're deaf," Peter continued, "but I know you understand me perfectly well. I can see it in your eyes. I don't know how you manage if you can't talk or sign."

Nick gave another shrug. He wanted to get on with things. Where did the man want him to swim? And why?

"It's like this," Peter said. "I'm a reporter. I write for a newspaper. You get that?"

Nick nodded for him to go on.

"I'm always on the lookout for unusual stories. Human interest stories. That's why I happen to know about the TTY and that's why I know some sign language. I picked it up when I was doing an article about a school for the deaf. The Dolan School. You know of it?"

Nick shook his head.

"It's pretty good."

Nick shifted his weight from one foot to the other. Was the guy going to carry on like this all morning?

Peter put a hand on Nick's shoulder. "What I wanted to ask you yesterday—except that you ran off—is if you can swim across the lake for me."

Nick's face fell. Drat! He was about to shake his head when he remembered his new orange raft. He smoothed the paper bag out on the floor and scribbled, "Can't swim over... am not 15... but have a raft."

Peter's face lit up. "Great! That's even better. I wasted most of yesterday looking for a boat. Can I borrow yours?"

Nick paused. He'd just gotten the raft. It was brand-new. He didn't want some stranger going off in it. He might never see it again. Besides, it might sink. Peter looked pretty big.

Nick shook his head and gestured to show that the raft was small.

"You're saying I won't fit in it?"

Nick nodded.

"Well then, can you go across for me?"

Nick paused before giving another nod.

"Today?"

Nick nodded again.

Peter glanced at his watch. "Suppose I meet you at the public beach at noon?"

Suddenly Nick was scared. No matter how friendly Peter was, or how easy he was to lip-read, he was a stranger. He hadn't even told Nick why he wanted him to go across the lake. Maybe it was a trap of some sort.

Peter's eyes studied him. "Look, it's no big deal, Nick. Your job will be easy. Call it a mission. A mission to save the lake."

Nick stared at him.

Peter looked around the store quickly before adding, "I think the lake is in danger."

Nick's eyes widened. The lake—his lake—was in danger! What was going on? His heart started beating faster. He opened his mouth to ask Peter what the problem was. Then he closed it. Then he opened it again. Should he ask or would Peter tell him?

Peter seemed not to notice Nick's agitation. He put a hand in his back pocket and drew his wallet out. "I'll pay you for going across the lake for me, Nick," he said. "In fact, I'll pay you right now."

Before Nick could shut his mouth, a $20 bill was in the palm of his hand and Peter was gone.

6

Twenty dollars! Nick's head spun as he raced home on his bike. Wags could barely keep up with him. Not only did he have a job, he'd earned his first money as a man of the water without even putting on his bathing suit! He'd never earned so much money in one shot before in his life.

Then Nick's mind switched to the lake. He was going to save the lake! He didn't even know what the danger was, but the feeling that this was an important job was strong and sure in him. He was so excited at the realization, he nearly rode right into a telephone pole!

Nick heard Peter's words as he raced up the walk to his apartment two at a time. "Your job will be easy. Call it a mission. A mission to save the lake."

A mission? What, exactly, was a mission? Mrs. Graves had used the word in speech therapy once because of the *s*'s in the middle. And one time his mother had taken out a video called *The Mission*. It was about a dark bearded priest who wanted to help a lot of half-naked South American natives. Nick had liked the wild tropical landscape and the foaming waterfalls, but even though the movie had closed captioning, he couldn't figure out the story and left the room before it was finished. His mother had cried over it.

Now she was in the kitchen making sandwiches. She greeted him with an angry look. Arrows were practically coming out of her eyes.

Nick frowned. What was it now?

She took his hand and slapped something into it. It was a wad of torn paper—the note she'd left for him.

Nick's mouth fell open. Oh no! He'd forgotten to call Mrs. Graves on his TTY to tell her he wasn't coming to therapy.

Nick found a pencil and scribbled on the back of an old envelope, "I'm sorry. I forgot."

She regarded him for a minute. Then she took the pencil and wrote in reply, "This can't go on for long or you *will* have to go away to a school for the deaf. Do you want that?"

Nick shrugged. He looked down at his feet as though thinking the matter over.

Nick's mother turned back to the counter. He took a peek to see what kind of sandwiches she was making. Cheese, tomato, and sprouts. He made a face. He could put up with most of the food from her health food store, but he did not like sprouts. They made him think of worms. How dare she sneak them in just because he wasn't talking! He tried to snatch them off the bread but his mother grabbed his wrists. They wrestled for a few minutes, then Nick broke away. She stuck her tongue out at him. He didn't do it back. He didn't even smile. He drew himself up as tall as he could and went into the living room. She wouldn't be treating him this way if she knew about his job—his mission.

Nick found the dictionary in the living room and opened it to the M section:

mission (mish-en): a special task assigned to a person or a group of people.

He liked the word. Looking at it there in the dictionary made him feel a bit like the way he felt when he was up in the pine tree. Big. Free.

Nick dug the $20 bill out of his pocket, opened it, laid it in the book right over the word, then shut the dictionary and put it back in its place on the shelf. He would add it to the wet-suit fund when he'd completed the mission. He could imagine his mother's eyes widening with surprise as he took the $20 bill out of the dictionary and handed it to her to put in the bank. She would realize he could get on in the world without therapy.

Nick got into his bathing suit, gathered his snorkeling equipment in his arms, and went into the kitchen to put his hearing aid in the drawer. To his surprise and annoyance, his mother was in her bathing suit, tying her madras wraparound skirt around her waist.

They glared at each other. He could see she was waiting for him to say something. He dropped his aid in the drawer and went to the front door.

Nick sank down in the front seat of the car, his arms folded tight across his chest as they drove to the lake. He didn't want her there. He wanted to do this mission all by himself. He had to! Why was she taking time off anyway? To make him talk? Wasn't she supposed to be working at the store?

Together they carried the rubber raft—with the oars, towels, snorkeling equipment, life preserver, and sandwiches inside—across the parking lot, down the beach, and into the lake. Wags raced on ahead. Peter wasn't in sight. The orange raft looked so good bobbing on the water, Nick almost forgot how angry he was at his mother. She talked with Amy for a while. Nick could see she was telling Amy about the orange raft.

When Nick's mother came back, she lifted the life preserver out of the boat and gestured for him to put it on.

Nick grimaced. Drat! He didn't need a life preserver. He *knew* how to swim.

Nick's mother pointed at Amy.

Nick looked at Amy.

Amy nodded and put her thumb up. That meant Nick had to wear the darn thing.

He put it on reluctantly. It was way too long. The collar nearly reached his earlobes. He would have made a fuss, but he knew this was the wrong time. He wanted his mother to hurry up and leave. He would take the ridiculous thing off as soon as he was out on the lake where no one could talk to him.

His mother wasn't in any rush, though. She took a towel and a sandwich from the raft, removed her skirt, and sat down on the sand.

Nick busied himself fitting the oars in the rubber locks. He snapped his fingers for Wags to hop in. She put one paw on the side of the raft and gave him an anxious look.

Nick snapped his fingers again. He'd never seen her taking so long to respond. Her slowness annoyed him. He wanted to get out on the water before Peter came. Otherwise his mother would see him with Peter. She'd always warned him not to talk to strangers. She would probably insist on meeting Peter and finding out all about him. If she did that, the mission wouldn't be his mission anymore. She might not even allow him to go on it if she knew about it.

Nick lifted Wags up and lowered her into the boat. She kicked as she came down and stood there wobbling on all fours like a tipsy sailor. Either she didn't want to go or she didn't like inflated rubber rafts. Nick got her to lie down. She popped up a second later. Again he made her lie down. Then he climbed in, settled down opposite her, and began rowing.

The orange raft skimmed along. It was awesome. Now Nick could go anywhere on the lake. He stopped about forty yards from the shore and looked back. His mother waved. He waved in response. Nobody was swimming. Like the day before, there were only a couple of little kids playing in the sand while their mothers chatted. Nick unwrapped his sandwich, removed the sprouts one by one onto the waxed paper, and let the boat drift while he ate.

Sprouts or no sprouts, Nick couldn't finish his lunch. He gave it to Wags, who still didn't want to lie down. Nick's head teemed with questions. What was wrong with the lake? What was the danger? He looked down into the water. It was clear. Clear enough for him to see the rocks at the bottom. It didn't look polluted.

He looked out over the calm, glassy water all around. There wasn't a ripple on the surface of the lake, and there weren't many clouds in the sky. Anyone would say it was a perfect June day. Maybe a little bit cool, but just about perfect. What did Peter know about the lake that Nick couldn't see with his eyes? The thought—Peter knew something he didn't know and the lake was in danger—made goose pimples pop up on Nick's arms.

When Nick glanced back at the beach, he saw Peter immediately. He was by the water's edge, not far from Nick's mother. He was wearing the shiny sunglasses. He waved.

Nick waved back. His mother responded. She thought he was waving to her. Then she stood and gathered up her stuff. At last she was leaving! She waved again and gestured at her watch. Nick knew she was telling him she'd be back later when she got out of work. He gave a thumbs-up sign.

Peter took his sunglasses off when Nick reached the shore. Wags jumped out quickly and shook herself.

"You're right," said Peter with a nod at the raft. "I wouldn't fit in that."

Wags wagged at Peter.

"You've got a neat dog there," Peter added. "We made friends yesterday."

Wags wagged some more. Nick took hold of her collar. He didn't like how well the two got along. Wags was *his* dog.

"I had a mutt like her when I was a kid. They're real smart."

Nick wanted to say Wags wasn't like any other dog in the world. She was more than smart, she was a genius of a dog. But he kept his mouth shut tight.

"Was that your mother who just left?"

Nick nodded.

"She's pretty."

Nick shrugged. His mother was thirty-four, way too old to be pretty.

"Is she deaf?"

Nick frowned and shook his head. Peter sure was nosy.

"You really can't talk or sign?" The concern was in Peter's eyes again.

Nick kicked at the sand with his foot. He was there for orders, not for chitchat or pity. He hated it when people got that concerned, "Are-you-OK?" look.

"I don't mean to bother you," said Peter. "When you're a reporter you get in the habit of asking questions. You want to know about people. You want to figure out why they are the way they are. It's like putting a puzzle together."

Nick gave another shrug.

Peter took a yellow box out of his pocket and squatted down. Nick saw it was a small disposable camera. He'd seen them in the drugstore and had thought he'd like to get one. One that was waterproof. When his mother told him how expensive they were to have developed, he'd changed his mind. The wet-suit fund came first.

Peter slid the camera out of the box and tore off the shiny wrapping paper. "Ever seen one of these?"

Nick nodded.

"This one is waterproof. You know how it works?"

Nick nodded again, though he'd never touched one before in his life.

"Let me show you, just to be sure. I want you to take it with you when you go across the lake," Peter said. "I want you to get me some pictures of those big old trees over there, and the swans and the ducks. And a couple of the public beach from the middle of the lake. You get that?"

Another nod from Nick to say he understood. He almost groaned out loud, though. All he had to do was take a bunch of pretty pictures. There was no swimming involved. No snorkeling. No diving, or gathering samples of sand or seaweed, or catching fish, or anything exciting.

Nick's face must have fallen, because Peter put a hand on his shoulder. "These photos are important. I need them for an article I'm writing."

Nick waited for him to say more.

"You know there's a convent over there?"

Nick nodded.

"That convent has protected the lake all these

years," Peter continued. "This lake is one of the few unspoiled lakes in Connecticut."

Peter let the words sink in before going on. "Now look, Nick, there's a man who wants to buy some of the land over there. He's a land developer. He's offering a lot of money. The nuns need the money. Got me?"

Nick nodded.

"The man says he'll only build one house, maybe two houses. I don't believe him. Not for a minute. I think he might have other plans. Yesterday I discovered he owns a club in Florida. He never mentioned this to anyone in town. It's a big fancy club with a golf course, docks, boats for waterskiing, the works. How do we know he isn't planning to build the same here? We don't. If we can let people know what's going on, maybe they'll find a way to help the nuns so they don't have to sell the land."

Waterskiers? Docks? A golf course? Nick blinked. He knew enough about the rain forests to know what could happen if the convent land was gobbled up by a developer. It would mean garbage, noise, gas in the lake. It would mean more and more boats. More and more people. It would be awful. He'd never get to camp under the willows or in the woods. What would happen to the deer? The birds? The fish?

Nick looked into Peter's eyes and gave one quick, fierce nod to show he understood.

67

Peter rumpled Nick's hair. "I knew you could help me."

Nick put a hand out for the camera.

Peter gave it to him. Then he stood up and pointed at his wristwatch. "The deadline for the article is 5:00. Can you get the camera back to me by 3:30?"

Nick looked at his own watch. It was almost 12:30. He'd better get going.

7

Peter held the raft while Nick and Wags got in. Then he gave them a firm shove and a good-luck wave.

Nick started rowing. It was hard going though, because Wags kept standing up and Nick kept pushing her back down. Every time she got up, the boat swung back and forth or tipped precariously to one side or the other.

When Wags popped up for the sixth or seventh time, Nick did something he'd never done before in his life. He raised his hand to hit her. He was not only angry, he was afraid. Afraid they would turn over and all the snorkeling equipment and the camera would wind up at the bottom of the lake.

Wags's ears went flat back against her head. She sat down without taking her eyes off Nick. Her face said, "I'll do what you want, but I don't like this situation at all."

Nick lowered his hand. He felt ashamed because he'd almost hit her. But wasn't it *her* fault? Next time he went out he wasn't going to take her. She could stay at the beach or swim along beside the boat if she wanted. But right now there was no time to lose, and she was going to have to sit still whether she liked it or not.

Nick picked up the oars again. The boat went faster.

When they were about halfway across the lake, Nick stopped to rest his arms. He'd been so busy trying to get Wags to be quiet he hadn't noticed that the surface of the lake was no longer smooth. A steady wind had come up, and the sky had turned hazy.

Nick looked back at the beach. There was only a handful of people. Amy appeared to be reading. Peter wasn't in sight. He'd told Nick he had to go back to his computer and would return at 3:30. For a moment, Nick wondered if the whole meeting with Peter had really happened. It could have been one of his daydreams. But no, it wasn't— there was the camera on top of his flippers.

Nick picked up the camera and turned it over. He was going to get as close to the willows as he could. He hoped the swans would be there. Or better yet, the deer. He could imagine a picture of the deer by the lake. Maybe it would even appear on the front page of the newspaper with the caption: **OUR LAKE IS IN DANGER!** Thinking about the photo made Nick wonder if his name would appear under the photos in the newspaper. His mother would flip out! She'd be so proud! She might offer to get him a waterproof camera of his own and pay for the developing. Wouldn't Mrs. Graves be surprised when she came across his name in the paper? He wouldn't point it out to her—he'd let her find it. And Aaron might see it. And the kids at school . . .

The rising wind brought Nick back to the present. It was a sharp wind with a chilly edge. For the first time since he'd put on the life preserver, he was glad for it. It was like a thick vest. He decided not to take it off after all. Then he remembered, Peter had asked for some photos of the public beach. Nick lifted the camera to one eye and took his first picture.

Right afterward, he realized that his bathing suit felt wet. Nick got onto his knees and felt his suit. It was wet. Dripping wet. His towel and snorkeling stuff were wet, too. He looked at Wags and frowned. Both of them were sitting in a shallow puddle. How could he have missed that?

How wet had Wags been when she had gotten into the boat? Had she gone swimming first and brought the water in on her fur? He wasn't sure, but he didn't think so.

He started rowing again.

Wags put one paw on the edge of the boat. She never took her eyes off Nick. She looked miserable. Nick ignored her.

Wags took her paw off the edge of the boat and wagged her stringy wet tail to get his attention.

Nick finally looked at her.

Her brown eyes were really pleading.

Darn the dog! She could be as persistent as his mother! Nick leaned over to give her a quick reassuring pat. As he did so he saw there was more water behind her. He gulped. There, on the side of the raft right behind Wags, was a hole. Panic hit him. Oh no! His brand-new rubber raft was leaking! That was what Wags had been trying to tell him. What was he going to do?

He glanced around, snatched up his mask, and started bailing. At first it seemed to help. Then more water seeped in slowly, steadily.

Wags stood up, nearly tipping the boat over. Nick hustled her into the bow of the boat, pushed her down and looked back at the public beach again. Should he go back or should he push on to the opposite shore? If he went back to try to fix the raft he wouldn't have enough time to take the photos. The leak looked like a slow one to him.

Nick sat down, grabbed the oars, and headed for one of the willows. He *had* to get the pictures. They were his mission.

Nick rowed and rowed. It was slow going, not only because the boat was getting heavier, but because of the waves. They got bigger and bigger. He rowed upwind, right into them. His bathing suit was soaked but the life preserver remained fairly dry and warm. He pulled as hard as he could at the oars while Wags sat facing forward, her ears flapping in the wind.

They were about twenty-five feet from the shore when the raft suddenly seesawed wildly. Nick swung around in time to see a dozen or more mallards flapping up and out from under long yellow-green willow hair. The ducks skimmed past Nick close to the surface of the water, their necks stretched out, their webbed feet held straight back against their bodies.

They'd been frightened by Wags, who had belly flopped into the lake and was paddling toward the shore.

Nick stared after them. There went his photos!

A second later, a mother swan swam out from under the willow, followed by three fluffy gray babies. Nick reached for the camera. Then he saw that Wags was going for the swans.

Nick lowered the camera. What did Wags think she was doing? She was headed for big trouble if she thought she could catch a swan. The mother swan's long white neck flattened out at Wags like the taut neck of a snake. She looked as though she was hissing.

Nick gave two quick hard claps and whistled.

Wags circled around and swam back toward the raft, her ears flat against her head.

Nick got a couple of photos of the swans as they moved on, downshore, in the direction of the boathouse. He didn't follow them because of Wags. He noticed, as he lowered the camera, that the boathouse was quite large and that all of the windows were shuttered. There were two large NO TRESPASSING signs on the lake side of the house.

Nick also saw that the brown growth that obscured the lower part of the house was a thicket of cattails. There were water-lily pads too, which meant there might be turtles. He squinted. Some of the reeds looked trampled. Was that a pathway through the cattails up to the house?

Nick's new orange raft was turning into a bathtub. He tucked the camera inside the life preserver against his chest, piled the snorkeling equipment in the bow, and slipped over the edge of the boat into the lake. The water came up over his knees.

The rocks were sharp underfoot after the sandy public beach. Nick towed the raft in. Then he dragged it out of the lake and up the stony shore to a grassy spot beneath one of the willows. Wags shook herself off and started zigzagging all around with lowered nose and an alert, upright tail.

Nick tipped the raft to empty it out. To his dismay, the hole was about the size of a dime. Had one of the dog's nails punctured the rubber? What could he do about it? He looked around. Rocks, brambles, old wood, grass, tangled bits of reeds, water lilies and duckweed. There wasn't anything he could use to patch up the raft. His watch read 1:10. How in the heck was he going to get the pictures and return by 3:30? Not only had Wags frightened all the birds away, she and Nick were stranded.

Nick decided to explore the shore area around the boathouse. He'd tell Wags to stay with the raft so she wouldn't scare off any more birds and he could take pictures. Then he'd swim back across the lake with the camera. He'd be going with the waves and would have his flippers. He was sure he could get back to the public beach by 3:30. He would figure out how to get his boat and the other stuff later. Wags would swim with him. It would be cold, but he knew he could do it. He'd be the first kid under fifteen to swim across the lake alone! His face got warm as he thought about it.

Nick clapped for Wags and gestured for her to stay by the boat. She looked disappointed, but did as she was told and lay down on the grass beside Nick's snorkeling equipment.

Camera in hand, life preserver still on, Nick made his way down the shore, hopping from rock to rock and climbing over fallen trees. He got a picture of some mallards but that was all.

When he reached the cattails, Nick saw that there *was* a path. The growth had been hacked back neatly. It had been done in such a way, though, that the path wasn't straight—it curved around into the heart of the thicket.

Curious, Nick followed the path. The earth was soft and muddy underfoot. He stopped as he recognized footprints in the mud. Faint human footprints. He squatted down and looked at them. His father had told him a little bit about reading animal tracks the last time he was in Maine. What could he read in a human footprint?

There were three different imprints. Two of the imprints were quite large. They looked as though they'd been made by heavy people wearing shoes or boots. The third set of prints was small and had a clover pattern in the middle. Nick knew the imprint must have been made with Vibram soles. He knew because his father had boots with the same clover pattern on the bottom.

The imprints led up the path toward the house and then back. The imprints that went in were older and fainter than the ones that came out. They puzzled Nick. Who would be going in and out? The nuns? In boots? Carlos? Maybe Carlos went fishing in the early morning or late evening.

Nick went on. The path began to curve again, this time toward the edge of the boathouse. He walked on the balls of his feet, softly, looking to the left and right. He stopped, rubbed his arms, and listened through his eyes. He felt strangely tense. There was nothing, nobody, only the wind bending the reeds and the clouds building up overhead.

Just before Nick reached the edge of the boathouse, he thought he saw something red out of the corner of one eye. He turned. Yes, there was something red under the reeds.

He stepped off the path, pushed past the cattails, leaned over, and looked. A red-pink feather about two and a half inches long lay on the mud. Nick picked it up. His heart sped up as he wiped it off. What kind of a bird would have such a bright feather? Not a cardinal—it was too pink. A scarlet tanager?

Something clicked in Nick's head a split second after he'd thought of the scarlet tanager. He remembered the newspaper photo in the pocket of his shorts at home. He could see the bird perfectly, lying limp in the hands of the police officer. His mouth fell open. Could it be? Could it possibly be the feather of a scarlet macaw?

8

Nick knew he ought to concentrate on getting the photos and starting back across the lake, but the feather held him there. It was so bright. It was brighter than anything he'd ever seen in Mrs. F.'s shop. A weird thought crossed his mind: the feather made him think of a knife that had been dipped in blood.

Nick slapped his leg. He had work to do. He couldn't let his imagination run wild.

But still, the questions came in a rush: Where was the bird it came from? What was the feather doing here under the cattails, beside a small lake in New England? How long had it been here?

Nick looked around carefully. Nothing. No bird. Just cattail and water-lily leaves, mud, snails, and a couple of painted turtles. If he hadn't found the feather, he would have been eagerly making mental notes on everything for his notebook. But now he felt disappointed, without knowing why. He certainly didn't want to stumble over a dead macaw.

Nick looked at his watch. It was almost 2:00. What about the pictures? He dodged the question. Were there more feathers up ahead? Where did the path go, anyway? He decided to take a quick look.

The path led in the direction of the boathouse. As he came closer, Nick saw how the house was built on the edge of a steep slope. He saw the dirty white, peeling paint, the old NO TRESPASS-ING signs nailed to the front, and the shuttered windows. There were six windows altogether, three up above and three down below. The first floor windows were almost entirely hidden by the trees that had grown up at the bottom of the slope. Nick saw, though, that those windows were connected by a narrow shelf with latticed iron sides that held wooden flower boxes.

The path ended at a mossy stone stairway built into the slope. Unruly bushes, trees, brambles, and poison ivy grew on both sides of the stairs. Although the boathouse looked neglected, the brambles had been cut back just enough so that a person could go up or down the stairs without getting scratched.

Nick went up the stairs, the feather still in his hand. There, at the top, was another path leading alongside the boathouse to the front drive. He noticed that the side windows weren't shuttered, but the shades were drawn all the way down.

He followed the path to the front drive. His heart gave a little leap as he recognized the blue-and-white pickup truck parked outside the front door. So this was where Carlos lived.

Nick looked around. An overgrown meadow bordered one side of the drive. It must have once been the lawn that had stretched down from the main house to the slope and on to the lakeside. Nick couldn't see the house—it was blocked from view by huge thick, gray-trunked beech trees with long, sweeping branches.

On the other side of the drive was an enormous fenced-in garden. Nick stepped across the dirt road to take a look. There were strawberries, rhubarb, and neat rows of lettuce, peas, spinach, and beans. He remembered the snow peas in the salad the night before. They'd probably come from here.

A hoe leaned against the wooden gate. A brown jacket had been thrown over the top of the gate. Nick recognized the jacket. Carlos always wore it over an old striped shirt. It looked to Nick as though the gardener had left his gardening for a couple of minutes and planned to return soon. Nick turned around and around. No Carlos.

Nick hesitated before going to the front door of the boathouse. He was sorry he'd been rude the day before. Maybe, if he really looked Carlos in the eyes, Carlos would see he was sorry and would be able to help him fix the raft. Or maybe he would be able to give Nick and Wags a ride back to the public beach.

Nick knocked once on the blue weather-stained door.

There was no response.

He tried two more times.

Then he put a hand on the doorknob. It turned. He pushed and the door opened into a large room.

Nick could see that the room must have been quite elegant at one time because of the high white ceiling and the large stone fireplace. But now it was shabby and unkempt. Wooden crates were piled in one corner, a stack of newspapers in another. Cardboard boxes were scattered all about. Rumpled clothing had been tossed onto the sofa and chairs. On a low table in front of the sofa were two dirty plates with forks. Two plates? Two forks? Half a dozen beer cans, too. Nick scratched his head. Hadn't his mother said Carlos had come to the United States alone?

Nick looked down. Right near his foot was a black duffle bag and a red backpack with a metal frame. He knew it was an expensive backpack.

He'd wanted one like it when he was in fourth grade and his mother had made a face and told him he'd better be happy with whatever he got. The Four Seasons Sport Shop didn't carry stuff like that backpack. You could only find them in special stores. What was it doing here of all places? How could Carlos have gotten it? Did the nuns hike around the convent wearing fancy backpacks? People who went trekking in the Himalayas used packs like that.

Nick stooped to turn the pack over and take a quick look at it, but drew his hand back quickly as though he'd been burned. Another red feather lay under the pack!

Nick drew the feather out carefully. It was shorter than the feather he'd found outside. But the color and shape of the two matched perfectly, like two leaves from the same tree.

Nick glanced around. His neck and shoulders felt awfully tight. He saw that the kitchen was right off the living room. Could there be a bird in there?

He stepped into the kitchen. The sink was piled full of unwashed pots and pans. A fishy smell hovered over the overflowing garbage can. The mess puzzled Nick. The garden outside looked neat and well cared for, but this—this was a real mess. Weren't the wooden crates of vegetables that Carlos brought to the health food store always packed carefully? Maybe Carlos didn't live in the boathouse and Nick was looking in the wrong place.

Nick turned to leave, but a light in the back hall off the kitchen caught his eye. Perhaps Carlos had gone down the back hall into the basement and Nick would find him there.

Shelves lined the small hallway. Tin cans were stacked on one shelf, boxes on another, cleaning detergents on a third. Things were neat here but—in the middle of the hall—Nick felt something gritty under his feet. He stopped to take a look. At first he thought it was sand, then he thought it was spilled rice or lentils. He rubbed the gritty stuff between his fingers and knew, as he did so, that it was seed. He saw a plastic bag that had fallen over on its side on the lowest shelf near his knee. There was hardly any light down there, but the shape of the bag was familiar. Nick lifted it to the lightbulb. It was birdseed, the exact same brand for cockatiels and parrots that Mrs. F. sold in her store.

Nick saw that the bag had been torn open at the side, rather than on top. That was why it was leaking. He twisted it a bit to close the hole. As he was putting it back, he saw another bag. And another. He counted nine bags of seed. Beside them on the bottom shelf, barely visible in the dim light, were six boxes with bottles of liquid vitamins.

Goose pimples popped up on Nick's bare arms and legs. He was scared stiff of being found there by the gardener. He knew without a doubt he was onto something big.

Nick rubbed his arms hard. No wonder Carlos seemed so nervous all the time. His mother was going to be pretty upset when she learned the guy was a thief.

Nick wanted to get out of that house—and fast. But where was the bird? By now Nick was convinced there was a scarlet macaw in the house and he had to find it. The feeling was so strong in him he couldn't ignore it. He *had* to see if the bird was alive and well.

Nick moved cautiously down the hall, afraid that somebody somewhere in the house might hear his pounding heart. He put both hands over the life preserver as if to muffle the sound.

There was only one door at the end of the hall. It was locked. Nick would have retraced his steps except for the smell. A musty ammonia smell hung in the air. He knew it was the smell of bird droppings and molting feathers. He knew it from Mrs. F.'s shop—he could have identified it anywhere.

There was a key in the lock. Nick took the key out and peered through the keyhole. He thought he saw wire. Chicken wire? Chicken wire inside a house?

Then something blue and red moved into Nick's line of vision. He could just make out part of the wing of a bird.

Nick quickly put the key back in the lock and

turned it. He opened the door a tiny bit and peeked in.

There was chicken wire. It was attached to the ceiling and hung down to the floor.

Nick pushed the door open a few more inches and gasped. There *was* a scarlet macaw in the house. And not just one—three of them!

9

The birds were unlike anything Nick had ever seen. They made him think of enormous, exotic tropical flowers from some National Geographic tape, except there were no jungle leaves in the background. Just shabby gray walls, harsh bare lightbulbs, and black shutters closed over the only window.

Nick dropped the feathers. His hands tightened into fists. These birds didn't belong here. They belonged outdoors—in the trees and the open sky.

The two huge macaws perched on top of the wooden crate were at least as long as Nick's arm.

Mrs. F's cockatiels and parrots would have looked like toys beside them. The third bird was on the rug, right below the crate. It didn't look good. In fact, Nick thought it was dead. The bird lay on its side, its eyes closed.

All of the birds had brilliant scarlet hoods, large white-and-black curving beaks, and creamy white masks around their eyes. Their hoods went down to their shoulders. Pale blue and blue-green wing feathers grew out from under their hoods. Long blue swordlike tail feathers jutted out behind them.

Neither of the scarlet macaws perched on the crate moved. Nick knew from the ruffled look of their feathers that they were waiting to see what he would do. He'd seen how Mrs. F.'s cockatiels raised their crests when strangers entered the store—in the same way that Wags's fur went up when she smelled something unfamiliar.

A corner of the room had been partitioned off with the chicken wire to make a cage for the birds. Nick shook his head. The macaws probably couldn't fly more than a foot without crashing into a wall, or a window, or the wire. He shook his head again. There was nothing for them to climb on. Mrs. F. would have had a fit! She wouldn't sell her parrots to people unless they understood the importance of providing plenty of room for the birds to exercise and play.

Nick inched closer. The birds shifted nervously. Nick froze. He didn't want to frighten them more.

Suddenly he felt a low thumping vibration. Where was it coming from? He swung around, stumbled, and nearly fell over. Carlos was sitting behind the door on a chair. A white gag was squeezed tight over his mustache and mouth. His arms were pinned behind his back. He'd been stamping the floor with his feet to get Nick's attention, even though his feet were tied together. His gray eyebrows shot up and down, making desperate signals.

Nick stepped back. What was happening here?

Carlos stamped his feet again. His eyes pleaded, "Help me!"

Nick struggled with the knot on the gag. He couldn't undo it, but was able to pull it down till Carlos's mouth appeared. The left side of his face was swollen and purple. His mustache and mouth moved a mile a minute.

Nick panicked. He couldn't understand. The words were all a jumble. Were they English or Spanish? He could see the gap where a tooth was missing, and he remembered his mother telling him Carlos had pulled out his own tooth.

Nick winced as he squatted down behind the chair. Carlos's wrinkled, weathered hands were all puffy; a cord cut into them. When he tugged at the cord, Carlos jerked his head back in pain. There were big knots. Impossible double knots.

Carlos stamped again.

"I'll . . . I'll get a knife," Nick whispered facing

him. Carlos frowned. He didn't understand.

Nick started for the door.

Carlos shook his head frantically. His mustache and lips moved. Another jumble of words poured out.

"I'll be back," Nick promised. "I won't leave you. I'll get a knife... or... " Nick remembered he had trouble making *s*'s. He moved two fingers through the air as though cutting with scissors.

Carlos shook his head. His mouth moved a bit more slowly.

"... shere ... four ... me ... "

Nick got a few words here and there but he couldn't fit them together. He gave a hopeless shrug. He felt a suffocating panic. He wanted to run out of the house and back to the lake. But Carlos needed help. The birds needed help, too.

"I ... I *will* come back," Nick stammered, inching his way to the door. One of the macaws flapped its wings wildly.

Carlos's mouth stopped moving abruptly. His eyes begged Nick not to go.

Nick stopped again. He *wanted* to help him. Couldn't Carlos see? Oh DRAT! Why couldn't they understand each other? Why couldn't they talk like everybody else?

Then Carlos's eyes moved up and down. They went down to Nick's wristwatch and up to Nick's face. Up and down, up and down.

Nick looked at his watch. It was 2:45. Was

Carlos asking for the time?

Nick showed Carlos his watch.

Carlos's eyes shifted swiftly from Nick's watch to the door, then back to Nick's face again. He frowned—his mustache frowned too. Carlos shook his head.

Someone is coming soon. Nick felt sure that was what Carlos was trying to tell him.

Nick took another step toward the door and Carlos shook his head again, even harder than before. Nick knew, like he knew when Wags was telling him she wanted supper or wanted to play, that Carlos did not want him to go out the door.

His shoulders and neck ached with tension. What should he do? *Who* was coming? What would happen?

One of the big macaws was on the floor now and had started pacing nervously. Back and forth, back and forth. Nick felt the scratchy movements of the bird's claws through his bare feet on the floor. The other macaw kept watch from the top of the crate.

Carlos jerked his head at the door.

Nick was confused. If Carlos didn't want him to leave, then what was he trying to tell him about the door?

Without taking his eyes off Carlos's face, Nick inched over to the door and put a hand on it. The gardener's eyes dropped quickly to the keyhole.

Get the key. The thought slipped easily into

Nick's mind.

He reached for the key and Carlos nodded.

Nick shut the door as quietly as he could.

Carlos nodded again and looked, first at the key in Nick's hand, and then at the keyhole.

Nick locked the door. Now they were locked in with the birds. Whoever was coming wouldn't be able to get in unless he—or they—broke the door down. Or—Nick glanced at the shutters—unless they forced their way in through the window.

Nick turned back to Carlos. The gardener was grinning. His dark eyes said, "We understand each other."

Nick couldn't smile, though. What should he do now? How could he untie Carlos? How would they get out? This was wilder, weirder, and more frightening than anything Nick had ever imagined. He'd crossed the lake to get a few pretty pictures, and here he was among prisoners!

Nick remembered the camera tucked under the life preserver rubbing against his chest. He took it out. There was no way he could get back to the beach by 3:30. What would Peter do? What time would his mother come? Would they connect? Nick was pretty sure neither of them would be able to see the orange raft under the willow tree from that far away. It might be hours before they started looking for him. What had he gotten into?

Carlos was stamping again. The grin was gone. His eyes were talking. They moved from Nick's face, to the camera, to the birds, to Nick. They did that once, then again.

Nick understood. *Take pictures of the birds.*

Nick scratched his head. Was there enough light?

Carlos stamped. *Hurry! Hurry! Hurry!*

Nick scrambled under the chicken wire. The macaw on top of the crate spread his wings full length and flapped as Nick stood up. For a second, the big bird looked like an enormous, angry, red-headed reptile. Nick could almost hear him hissing.

Nick dropped to the floor, one arm up to ward off an attack. After one long minute, the bird lowered its wings and started to preen itself. The other macaw watched.

Nick glanced back through the wire at Carlos. The man's mustache was bunched up and his lips were puckered. He was talking to the birds in whistles. They seemed to like whatever he was telling them, because they relaxed and ignored Nick.

Nick moved cautiously to open the shutters. He needed to let in more light for the camera. He knew the window was also his only means of escape.

The window was stuck; it only opened halfway. It probably hadn't been opened for years. Three hooks held the black shutters closed. Fortunately Nick could reach them and they weren't too rusty. When he pushed them open, afternoon light poured in. He saw that the sky had clouded over completely. One of the narrow flower boxes he'd noticed from the ground was directly in front of him. Nick took a quick peek down. The mossy stairway was about ten feet below, to the right.

Carlos stamped his feet again. His eyes darted from the door to Nick, urging him to hurry.

Nick closed the window. Tempting as it was to let the birds out, he knew they probably wouldn't survive for long in the Connecticut climate.

The light wasn't great but Nick took hasty pictures anyway. He got as many different angles as he could. Click. Click. Click. He took a couple of shots of Carlos in the chair, too.

Suddenly the floor was vibrating again. Carlos stared at the door, as though hypnotized. The knob was turning back and forth. Someone was trying to get in!

Go! Carlos nodded at the window.

Nick couldn't move. What did the Carlos expect him to do? Fly out like a bird? Throw the camera in the shrubs? Dive into the trees? He couldn't jump to the ground. He'd break his legs!

Another kind of thumping had started up. It came from the door. It was angry, insistent.

In his panic, Nick almost missed the message. Carlos looked down at the floor, then up at the window. Down and up, down and up went his eyes.

Nick followed the movements. He saw the blanket on the floor inside the cage. It was a filthy brown thing covered with feathers, fluff, seed, and droppings.

Out the window...

In a flash, Nick understood. Of course! He should have noticed the blanket. He would use it to lower himself from the window.

He jammed the camera back inside the life jacket and dragged two crates off the blanket. He quickly knelt beside the motionless macaw on the floor. One dark beadlike eye opened. It was alive! Nick's hands trembled as he slid them gently under the soft body. It was amazingly light. He wanted to hold the bird against his cheek to listen for its heartbeat, but instead he put it back down on the floor, its back against the wall.

The other birds watched Nick carry the blanket to the window, pile it on top of the flower box, and scramble out through the tight opening. For the first time in his life, Nick was glad he was small.

As Nick turned to close the window, Carlos's brown eyes met and held his. Nick heard the cry in them: *Help me! Save me.*

Nick turned away quickly. He couldn't nod; he couldn't promise anything. He slid the window shut and turned to face the ten-foot drop in front of him.

10

The ironwork holding the flower boxes to the side of the house had a pattern of arrow-shaped leaves. Nick realized the leaves could be used as hooks to hold the blanket. He fastened one end the blanket to the leaf-hooks and threw the other end over the edge. It hung straight down, ending about four feet from the ground.

Nick turned onto his stomach and inched his way backward over the flower box. The wind tugged at his hair and the ironwork scraped at his legs. Then he grabbed the sides of the blanket with both hands and slipped over the edge.

For a second he dangled beside the house like a mountain climber clinging to the side of a hill. Then he slid down—not smoothly, but in jerks. When Nick thought he'd gone far enough, he let go of the blanket, jumped, and landed near the top stair.

Whew! He'd done it! He was free! Nick wanted to let out a whoop, but he didn't dare. Anything could happen. He couldn't stop being cautious just because he was out of the house.

Nick ran down the mossy steps into the thicket of reeds. The cold mud felt wonderful underfoot. He took two turns through the cattails and came to an abrupt stop.

There was a boat blocking the way—a small gray dinghy with an outboard engine resting inside against the rear seat. It was the kind of boat the local fishers used. How had it gotten here?

Nick saw the footprints circling the boat. Fresh footprints. He saw the clover pattern in the center of one of the smaller imprints. He could almost feel the hairs on the back of his neck standing up, because he knew the boat had been carried up from the lake and hidden among the reeds. He was sure that the winding path through the cattails had been cleared so whoever used it could have secret access to the boathouse.

Nick spun around nervously, half expecting to find someone standing behind him. No one. He could barely see one of the black shutters of the window he'd escaped from, hidden behind the treetops. Maybe he could use the boat to get back to the public beach?

Nick tugged and pushed at the boat. It wouldn't budge. There was no way he could get it into the lake by himself. Two or three people must have carried it up. Two or three people . . . Nick slipped past the boat and ran on.

Raindrops hit his forehead as he reached the lake. Was a thunderstorm coming? Darn! He had a big enough job in front of him without having to worry about lightning while swimming.

The waves broke against his legs and chest. He squinted across the water; the clouds and mist were so low he couldn't see across to the public beach. Nor were there any boats in sight. Nick glanced at his watch. It was 3:45. Only 3:45? It seemed like a couple of days had passed since Peter had pushed him off from the public beach in the orange raft. Was Peter waiting for him? Would Peter come looking for him?

Nick headed for the willow, Wags, the raft, and his flippers. Back over the rocks, the fallen tree trunks and the brambles. It was slippery going. The rain was coming down harder now. Nick planned as he went. Should he swim across the lake with or without the life preserver? He knew he would swim faster without it, but the waves were quite high. And the camera—how was he going to get that back? Tucked inside the life preserver against his chest, or what? The camera had better be as waterproof as Peter had said!

Nick clapped twice for Wags.

There was no sign of her.

Nick clapped again.

Nothing.

He went on. Where was Wags? Had she wandered off? Had something happened to her?

Even before Nick reached the grassy spot under the old willow, he knew Wags wasn't there. What really startled him, though, was that the orange raft—and his flippers, snorkel, mask, and towel—were gone too. Everything. Even the waxed paper his sandwich had been wrapped in. Nick turned around and around in bewilderment while the rain beat down on him. There wasn't a trace of anything.

Nick leaned against the willow to get his bearings. Was he in the right place? Wasn't the flattened area on the grass the place where the raft had lain? Had Peter been here?

Nick was so preoccupied with the disappearance of Wags, the raft, and the swimming gear that he didn't see the hooded figure right away. He gave a gasp when he looked up. Someone was coming down the shore. Someone in a blue windbreaker and jeans with fuzzy brown hair. Nick realized it was a woman because of the bright orange lipstick on her mouth.

As the woman came closer, Nick saw that she

was very, very tanned. Her tan made the orange lipstick really stand out. She looked as though she'd been in the Caribbean.

Nick's mouth fell open.

She smiled and waved.

Nick didn't respond.

She hopped gracefully from stone to stone and onto the grass just a few feet from Nick.

"I've been looking for you," she said. "Had trouble with your raft, didn't you?"

Nick nodded. Her lip movements were easy to read. The orange lipstick helped with that.

"I took your raft up to the road," she continued. "I'll take you home."

Nick stared at her. What road? The road that led to the convent? Was she a nun? He couldn't believe she was a nun with all that lipstick and the tan.

"I have the mask and flippers."

Nick scratched his head but still did not respond. Who was she? She looked nice enough—she was still smiling—but there was something about her that made him uneasy. He couldn't pinpoint what it was that bothered him.

"We've got everything."

Nick frowned. What about Wags? And who did this lady mean when she used the word "we"? He glanced around quickly but didn't see anyone else.

The woman tightened the hood about her face. Nick saw the impatience in the way her fingers moved. "Look," she said, "I haven't got all day. Your parents are worried. I told them I'd bring you home."

Nick's mother *and* father were looking for him! He almost grinned.

"They're very worried . . . "

But Nick didn't respond. Something didn't feel right.

Then it dawned on him that what she was saying didn't make sense. How could his father have gotten to Connecticut so quickly? His father would have to drive two hours through Maine just to get to the airport to come to Connecticut.

The woman was no longer smiling. "Let's go," she said.

Nick saw the hardness in her eyes. Her bright orange mouth could put on a fake smile but there was no smile in her eyes. They were cold and scheming.

As she stepped toward him, Nick saw the boots on her feet. Vibram hiking boots! The boots with the clover on the sole.

Nick drew back against the tree. He gestured at his ears and shook his head.

She stopped and stared at him. "What? What did you say?"

He gestured some more.

"He's deaf." She spoke to herself, not to him.

She regarded Nick for a second then she looked down the shore, waved and shouted, "He's

100

deaf—and dumb. Real dumb. I don't think we need bother with him."

Nick followed her glance. Someone else was on the shore near the path that led through the reeds. It looked like a man. A stocky man in a dark mackintosh and boots. He was shouting.

The woman said something to the man that Nick couldn't get. She tossed her head before taking another step toward Nick. Her orange mouth was set in an angry line. Her hard eyes were like dull, unpolished stones.

Nick stepped back, his hands in fists. The liar! She *hadn't* spoken with his mother. She *didn't* know anything about him. And she'd called him dumb!

Dumb? He wanted to punch her right in the mouth. He wanted to yell, "I AM NOT DUMB! WHO DO YOU THINK YOU ARE?" But he did nothing, said nothing, kept his face blank. It took all of his self-control to keep quiet. He knew, from the boots, that she was mixed up with everything he'd found in the boathouse. It might be best for him, Carlos, and the birds, to let her think he was deaf and dumb and couldn't understand what she was saying.

"Come on, boy," she said as though Nick was a stray dog.

She put out a hand to take hold of his arm, but he was too quick. He slipped past her, ducked down under the willow tree and jumped onto the rocky shore. He was too scared to feel the sharpness of the stones underfoot.

A second later he was in the lake swimming. Swimming like he'd never swum before.

11

The life preserver was a deadweight on Nick's body even though it helped him to keep his head above the waves. The camera kept slipping around inside the life preserver over his chest and stomach. If only he had his flippers! Then his legs could do the hard work while he held onto the camera with one hand. He knew that the photos—if they came out—would be important evidence that Carlos and the scarlet macaws were in danger.

Nick looked back. The woman was standing on the shore shouting at the man. The man was shouting, too, and waving at Nick. Nick had to grin. They looked silly. What was he supposed to do? Wave back? The grin turned into a frown. Where was Wags? What had they done with his dog? Was she locked up somewhere in the boathouse? Was she alive? Would he ever see her again? Nick gritted his teeth, turned, and swam on.

Nick still couldn't see the public beach because of the fog. It slid past him and on down the lake like a phantom train on its way to a far-off country. Within minutes the fog had cut him off from all land. The boathouse, the tanned woman with the orange lipstick, and the man further down the shore were gone—swallowed up in the rain and the grayness.

The wind had quieted down quite a bit but the surface of the lake was still choppy. Thank God it wasn't a thunderstorm! The rain was cold, as cold as the lake. Nick decided that if he ever did any kind of training in the future for scuba diving, it would have to include sitting in a deep, icy cold bath with a cold shower running at the same time.

To keep his mind off the cold, Nick thought of his mother as he swam. Sure, he got angry at her for pressuring him to join the Boy Scouts, make friends, and work on his speech. But she really was pretty cool. And she knew Spanish—where'd she ever learned Spanish? He'd have to ask her. That made him think of how she'd wanted to help Carlos. Nick could understand it now. She cared about people the way he cared about animals. Nick's throat began to sting as he realized she'd been right; he'd been jealous of Carlos. As if his mother's attention belonged to Nick only. Now all that seemed silly. He wanted to help Carlos, too.

The going was slow. Nick had never known swimming to be such a drag, a chore. And he thought he wanted to be a deep-sea diver! His legs were like lead blocks, his arms ached, his neck felt as though it might snap from being held at an odd angle because of the life preserver. Nick imagined his mother, Peter, Amy, and the police talking about him at the public beach. They'd better be there! They *had* to be there!

Nick glanced around and sucked in a mouthful of water by mistake. He spluttered and coughed. What if the man and the woman came after him in the dinghy? The boat could go right over him! He might not even see it coming! He could picture it bearing down on him. He could see the mean look in the woman's eyes and the smile on her orange lips turning into a sneer. The pictures were so vivid Nick turned this way and that, straining to see. Nothing but clouds, mist, rain, water. Nothing but fog with the light growing dimmer and dimmer. If only he could hear! If he could hear, he would know if they were coming and would be able to dive down under the water out of sight.

Nick began to feel dizzy and disoriented. Which way had he been swimming? Which way was the beach? He certainly didn't want to swim and swim and wind up back at the boathouse! That would be awful!

Nick shut his eyes. All the excitement, the suspense, and the anxiety that had been packed into that one wild day suddenly caught up with him and washed over him like a great wave. He was cold. So cold. His head swirled around and around, faster and faster.

Something poked at Nick's face.

Alarmed, he opened his eyes.

The fog was thicker, darker. Misty shapes hovered around him. Waves? Clouds? Where was he? What was going on?

The cold heaviness of his body told him he was in the lake. All he knew was that he wanted to be left alone. He wanted to go to sleep.

The poking continued. It forced him to think, to figure out where he was.

He was lying face up, the back of his head resting on the life preserver, his arms outspread. He could feel the tight, wrinkled skin on the tips of his fingers and the back of his scalp. His legs were weighing on him, pulling him downward. His mouth felt puffy, swollen.

A nudge at his ear.

Nick lifted a hand to his ear. Had he fainted? Was some animal trying to take a bite of him?

Some animal that assumed he was dead, a free-floating meal. Was it a rat?

It was at his arm now. His arm muscles, though numb, tensed.

Then something rough brushed against Nick's cheek.

A flicker of hope shot through Nick. Wags? He was afraid to even think it might be his dog. But he knew the sandpapery touch of her tongue on his skin by heart.

Nick turned his head slowly, ever so slowly, and looked. There were two dark eyes and a black nose bobbing up and down in front of him, urging him to get going.

"WAA—GS?" He hiccuped out her name.

Her eyes narrowed into a smile. She looked more like a seal than a dog with her wet ears plastered flat back against her head. Nick almost laughed—he knew she was trying hard to wag but couldn't because she was in the water.

Nick put an arm around her and tried to hug her while she paddled frantically to stay afloat. She was real! She was okay! They were together again!

Questions buzzed in Nick as warmth from the dog's presence seeped into him. Where'd she come from? How had she found him?

Wags poked and clawed at Nick's arm. "Let's go!" her eyes begged. "I want supper."

It was after 4:30. Nick felt the bump on his chest. The camera was still there. He flexed his fingers, then his arms, then his legs. He tried to connect with his body all the way down to the tips of his toes. Everything was cold and heavy.

He looked around, forcing himself to focus outward, to think about something other than his body. The surface of the lake was almost calm. The rain had stopped. An outline of trees appeared, disappeared, and then reappeared in the distance. Land! It was closer than he'd realized.

Nick judged he was more than halfway across the lake. But which shore was he looking at? The trees were pines. He'd always thought he knew the shoreline pretty well, but these pines didn't look at all familiar.

Wags poked at Nick's cheek again.

Nick knew they both had to get out of the lake—and soon—no matter which side he was looking at. He started swimming. Wags went on ahead.

After a few minutes Nick stopped. A movement in the distance had caught his attention. A dark shape was gliding over the water past the trees.

He squinted: It was a boat. He could just barely make out two dark figures standing, leaning forward, peering out ahead. Two dark figures—one tall and one short. It didn't look too good. He could almost see the woman's hard eyes searching for him.

"Here, Wags!"

She circled around and paddled back to him.

Nick put a hand on her collar. He wasn't going to let her out of sight or reach!

The boat glided downshore into the mist. Then it reappeared going in the opposite direction. Nick was sure it was combing the surface of the lake, looking for him. If he could figure out how long it took for the boat to make one run down the lake, he might be able to slip past it to the shore.

Suddenly a white light flashed out over the water. It swept right over and past Nick.

It happened so quickly Nick couldn't do anything but blink.

A second later the light came again.

Then again.

There was no time to dunk, no time to figure out what to do. The light was on him now. It was growing brighter and brighter. It was boring into him, blinding him, the way the headlights of a car paralyze a rabbit.

Nick knew they'd seen him. They were coming. Who were they? What would they do? The dog clawed frantically at the life preserver as Nick pulled her close. His teeth began to chatter uncontrollably.

Then the light dropped abruptly and shone on the surface of the water.

Nick smelled gasoline. The boat had stopped about five feet from them.

Nick still couldn't see who was in it because of the bright light. But Wags knew. She was squirming this way and that way. She was squirming the way she always did when Nick's mother came home.

12

Hands grabbed hold of Nick and hauled him out of the lake. His mother's arms went around him tight and firm. He felt her warm cheek against his cheek. A tall figure loomed up behind her. Peter. His hair looked wild, his eyes anxious. So Nick's mother and Peter had met.

Two other people—police officers in blue uniforms whom Nick had never seen before—were there too. One was at the engine, the other held the search light.

Nick's mother wrapped a towel round him. "Thank God you're alive!" There was just enough light for him to get the words on her lips.

"Mum . . . "

She was smiling and crying both at once.

"Waa-gs . . . " Nick chattered. "She shh-aved me . . . . "

Nick's mother held him tight while the others fished for Wags.

The boat rocked this way and that as Wags came in and tried to shake herself.

"Where's the raft?" Nick's mother asked.

"Gone . . . " He was too cold to be able to say more.

Nick's mother rolled her eyes. "Why'd I ever get it?"

Nick clutched at the life preserver as his mother fumbled with the zipper.

"The camm-rra . . . "

His mother put a hand over his lips to tell him to relax and be quiet.

The camera slipped to the floor of the boat as the life preserver was peeled off.

Nick lunged for the camera.

Peter got it first. He squeezed Nick's shoulder gently to tell him everything was okay.

"Carr-los . . . " Nick chattered as his mother pulled a sweatshirt over his head and guided his arms into the sleeves.

Nick's mother frowned. She hadn't understood him. She hugged Nick close as the police officer started up the engine.

Nick broke away. He bit his lip, looked at her and willed the chattering to stop. "Car-los," he shouted. "WE HAVE TO HELP CAR-LOS!"

Nick's mother still didn't understand. It was as though *she* was deaf, not him. What was the matter with her? Why was she so slow?

The boat jerked forward.

Nick waved his arms wildly. "Mum, stop, STOP!"

The boat stopped abruptly.

Peter bent over close so Nick could see his lips. "What's the matter, Nick?"

Everyone was staring at him, waiting. Maybe they all thought he had hypothermia and was delirious.

"It's Carlos ... " Nick tried again.

"Carlos?" Nick's mother asked. "You mean the man who brings vegetables to the health food store?"

Nick nodded hard.

"I thought you said Carlos. What about him?"

"He'z-tied-up-in-the-oathouse-we've-got-to-help-im."

"Whoa!" She put both hands up. "Slow down. What boathouse?"

Nick swallowed and said the words as slowly and clearly as he could. "The boathouse across the lake. There're birds, too, sharlet macaws."

"Scar-let macaws?" She corrected him.

Nick nodded some more. At last, she was hearing him!

"Parrots?"

More nodding.

"What are scarlet macaws doing over there?"

Nick shrugged. "One of them looks shick, real shick. . . . "

Peter tapped at Nick's arm to get his attention. "How big are these birds, Nick?"

Nick spread his arms wide.

Peter looked excited. "I did an article for the paper about a scarlet macaw. Do the birds have reddish heads and blue wing feathers?"

Nick nodded and stared at Peter. *Peter* had written the article that was in his shorts pocket!

"How many did you see?"

Nick held up three fingers.

Peter blinked with surprise.

"Carlos is with them," Nick put in. "They're locked in the boathouse."

Nick's mother, Peter, and the police were all talking at once now.

Nick tugged at his mother's arm. "Mum, there's a woman . . . "

"Tell us everything," she said. "And go slow."

Nick told them about his escape from the window, the gray boat, the woman with orange lipstick, and the other person on the shore. He could see that the police couldn't understand most of what he was saying, but his mother and Peter seemed to be following.

"Yikes!" Peter said when Nick had finished.

"Where is this woman?" Nick's mother looked ready to punch someone.

Nick shrugged. All he knew was that he'd fainted or something and Wags had poked him awake.

Peter talked with the police, trying to decide what to do. Nick looked up at his mother.

"They'll take us back to the beach, Nick. Then they'll check out the boathouse."

"But Mum . . . we've got to go there *now!!*"

"No sir! You're going home to a hot bath and a cup of soup!"

"Mum, I'm . . . I'm fine. I know where to go. I can show them."

"Nick, do you have any idea what *I've* been through today? It took the police forever to get this boat. I thought you'd drowned. Enough is enough!"

Nick took her hand in his. "Mum, *please!* I've got to help Carlos. I'll do anything you want . . . . I'll go to therapy . . . . "

Peter interrupted them then. Nick knew, from the way his mother's hand tightened in his, that Peter was putting in a word for him.

Nick's mother's eyes narrowed to pinpoints. "Well," she said turning to Nick, "if you're going, I'm going. I'm not going to let you out of my sight."

The engine started up again. Peter passed a

water bottle and two candy bars to Nick. Nick broke up one of the bars and fed it to Wags. His mother raised her eyebrows as he wolfed down the other. The soup was going to have to wait until later.

The clouds were almost gone. The dark shoreline was faintly visible. A thin mist hung in the air like steam hovering over an uncovered pot. Nick felt the tightness in his arms and neck as the pale exterior of the boathouse came into view. No lights were on. Was Carlos still in the back room? Nick couldn't see the window he'd escaped from.

Nick led the way through the thicket of reeds. He kept expecting to come upon the gray boat, but there was no sign of it. Baffled, Nick looked here and there among the cattails. The boat was gone. Mud had been scraped over the boot marks.

When they came to the mossy stairs, Nick looked up. *All* of the shutters on *all* of the windows were drawn. He sucked his breath in quickly. The blanket was gone too! Someone had gotten into the room and had covered up all traces of his escape. Were Carlos and the birds still there?

One of the police officers went up the stairs first. Nick followed, one hand on Wags's collar.

The blue-and-white pickup truck was still parked near the front door. One of the police officers checked it out. The keys were in the ignition.

Peter went with the police to the front door. Nick's mother drew Nick back by the stairs.

Peter shone a flashlight on the door while the police knocked. Nothing happened. Someone tried to open the door. It was locked.

The men talked together. They came over to Nick and his mother.

"You're sure Carlos was tied up?" Peter asked.

Nick nodded hard. He took them back by the mossy stairs and showed them the window he'd escaped from. "Call him," Nick begged.

Nick's mother, Peter, and the police all called and listened.

Nick saw from their faces that they didn't hear anything. What had happened to Carlos? What about the bird he'd held in his hands? His throat stung.

The police asked Peter a question which Peter passed on to Nick.

"Where's your raft?"

Nick shrugged. "I don't know. Shomeone took it."

"Could it have sunk?"

Nick nodded. "It had a hole." He showed the size of the hole with his fingers.

"Nick, could the raft have sunk in the middle of the lake?"

Nick nodded again, puzzled. What did the raft have to do with Carlos?

"Your mother told the police you were upset and hadn't been talking. Is that right?"

Nick gave a little shrug and looked at his

mother. She said something that he couldn't get.

"You *were* upset, weren't you?" Peter asked, for the police.

Nick gave an impatient nod. What a waste of time the questions were!

The adults went on talking.

As Nick watched the police, he suddenly knew that they didn't believe him. He could see it in their eyes when they looked at him. They probably thought he was being a smart aleck, making up stories, trying to get attention. Or else they thought he was dumb.

"Mum . . . ?" He tugged at his mother's arm.

She turned to him.

"It's true, Mum, honest, I shwear it's true."

She put a finger on his lips, telling him to be quiet.

Nick brushed her hand aside. "I didn't make this up. We've got to get in. If Carlos and the birds are in there . . . "

She put an arm around him. Nick ducked out from under her arm. She *had* to believe him. If she didn't believe him, he was never going to talk to her again in his entire life.

"Look," Nick's mother told him, "we can't go in the house. We have to go to the police station. There will be more questions."

Nick groaned. More talk. Why couldn't they check out the windows or get a key from the nuns? If they had a rope he'd climb back up the side of the house. He'd go down the chimney if they wanted.

Then he remembered the camera. "Mum, I took pictures in there. The cam-era . . . "

Peter's eyebrows went up. He dug the camera out of his jacket pocket and looked at it. "This could be the proof we need," he said. "We'd better get it to the lab. And fast!"

13

How many times had Nick crossed the lake that day? Too many times, he decided.

Despite his frustration, Nick dozed off in the boat as he sat between his mother and Peter. Wags, curled up at Nick's feet, slept too.

A police car with flashing orange and white lights was parked on the beach. There was an ambulance, too. Nick caught a glimpse of the lifeguard's frightened face as he, his mother, and Wags got into the police car. Peter waved at them and made a dash for his Honda. He was going straight to the lab with the camera.

Nick's mouth fell open when he came into the lobby at the police station. There was Mrs. F., sitting on a chair beneath the clock! A pair of reading glasses balanced on the end of her nose as she scanned a pile of papers.

"Mrs. F.!"

She looked up. "Nick Wilder, what are you doing here?"

"I found the shuff that was sholen from your shore . . . . " The words came out in a jumble.

Mrs. F. removed her reading glasses.

"I found shome shar-let macaws," Nick hurried on. "*Three* of them!"

Nick's words transformed the pet shop owner. There was no question she'd understood everything he'd said.

"WHERE are they?" she asked getting to her feet. "WHO has them?"

"The boathouse, Carlos . . . " Nick didn't know where to start.

Nick's mother turned his face to hers. "Slow, slow, Nick. The police chief is listening."

Nick swung around. Five police officers stood behind his mother. He didn't know which one was the chief. All he knew was that he had to speak as slowly and clearly as he could. So much depended on it. He turned back to Mrs. F. He knew *she* wouldn't interrupt him if he didn't say every word just right.

When Nick had finished, Mrs. F. grabbed the

papers off her chair with both hands and waved them in the air. She looked like a bird flapping its wings.

"I told you something was going on!" She spoke over Nick's head to the police. "I told you and you paid no attention!"

Mrs. F. shoved the papers at Nick. "Look!"

Nick and his mother looked.

The papers were photocopies of newspaper articles. The solid black headlines jumped out at Nick:

Disco Owner Pays $5,000 for Smuggled Bird
Parrot Smugglers Evade Sting
Parrot Smugglers Suspected in Shooting Death

The articles came from newspapers in Texas, Florida, and New York. There was a photo of ten scarlet macaws with their beaks taped, lying in a tight row like sardines in a tin. Captions said that all of the birds had died of suffocation. There was also a photo of an ice-cream truck. Amazon parrots had been found stuffed inside the four hubcaps and behind the headlights.

Nick felt sick. He turned to his mother and they stared at each other. So, he'd stumbled into a bird-smuggling ring! Wow! What would have happened if the woman with the orange lipstick had lured him back to the boathouse?

Mrs. F. gestured at Nick. "A federal investigator sent me these photos. You recognize any of the faces?" She passed him a packet of pictures.

Nick shook his head as he went through the first five. They were all of unfamiliar men. When Nick came to the sixth picture, he almost dropped it. The photo showed a woman in a public terminal making her way through a crowd. She was tanned, dressed in preppy shorts and sneakers, and wore dark glasses and a fancy pack on her back.

"That's her! That'sthepack shaw . . . It's red . . . " Nick couldn't slow down.

Mrs. F. gave one quick grim nod. "She smuggled macaws out of Brazil in that backpack. She drugged them so they wouldn't make any noise."

"How?" Nick remembered the listless macaw he'd picked up.

"Gave them aspirin or alcohol."

Nick's mother asked Mrs. F. a question.

"She came to my store about a week ago," Mrs. F. answered, waving the photograph Nick had picked out. "She looked around carefully. She was a stranger, no one from here—I know my customers the way I know my pets. My store was broken into over the weekend. I got this picture yesterday—I recognized her right away."

Nick frowned. "Why didn't she buy the bird sheed? Wouldn't that have been easier than breaking in?"

"Good thinking!" Mrs. F. clapped her hands. "You could be a detective, Nick. The woman needed the seed and the medicines, but what she was really after were the bands. That's why the store was turned upside down. She wanted us to think it was vandalism."

"Ahhh!" said Nick. He knew no bird could be sold without a metal band, like a bracelet, on its wrist. That was the proof that a bird had either been born and raised in captivity or had passed successfully through quarantine when entering the country. And the bands weren't ordinary bits of metal; they had numbers on them.

"Did she get them?"

Mrs. F. gave another quick grim nod. Nick understood then why she'd been so angry after the break-in. The smugglers really knew their business.

There was a lot of talk going on. Some of the police had left. Others had joined them. The papers and photos were passed around. Mrs. F. was going full steam. Nick's mother turned to him.

"You want to go home?"

Nick shook his head.

"I don't either," she admitted. "Not till we know about Carlos."

"And the birds," Nick added.

Forty minutes later, a police car with flashing lights pulled up outside the front door. Two police officers and a woman in a gray outfit with a white cloth over her head got out. Nick knew without asking that she was a nun. Her face was white and tense.

Ten minutes later, another car with flashing lights arrived. Nick grabbed his mother's arm as

Carlos emerged from the back door. As Carlos came in the lobby flanked by two police officers, he caught sight of Nick and a happy grin spread over his face.

Nick's mother stepped forward and addressed Carlos in Spanish. Nick watched while she helped the gardener answer questions from the police. Nick couldn't follow what was being said, but he saw how Carlos relaxed as the questioning proceeded.

Nick felt a tapping at his shoulder and swung around. There was Peter, two cameras hanging from his neck, a pad in one hand, and a pencil in the other.

"Your mother's great!"

Nick nodded in agreement.

"I never knew what I was getting you into," Peter said. "I feel terrible about it. What if . . . "

Nick didn't wait for him to finish. "Did the pictures come out?"

Peter nodded. "Haven't printed them up yet. The negatives were enough for the police to act on."

"The birds . . . ?"

"Gone."

Nick's face must have fallen because Peter squeezed his shoulder gently. "You were incredible, Nick! If you hadn't found the birds, we wouldn't know what was going on. Now the police know smuggling can happen even here in this town. They know what to look for."

Nick gave a little shrug. He wanted to see the scarlet macaws again, especially the one he'd held in his hands. Would it survive all the rough treatment?

Peter tapped at his arm again. "I think you've saved the lake, Nick."

"How?"

"This story will be on the front page tomorrow. It'll make people think about the lake, the convent, the wildlife."

"We can go home now," Nick's mother said joining them.

"What about Carlos?" Nick asked as Carlos passed them with a little wave on his way out to the police car.

"The police are taking him to the hospital for a checkup. He didn't pull his tooth out, Nick—he was beaten."

"But . . . ?"

"You want to know how he ever got into this mess, right?"

Nick nodded.

"The smugglers told Carlos he could make a lot of quick cash if he took care of the macaws while they expanded the black market. They met Carlos in California when he was looking for work and followed him here. The woman spoke Spanish. She saw how good Carlos was with the birds. She wanted him to breed macaws in the boathouse."

"But they beat Carlos and tied him up."

"That was later, after Carlos saw the birds when they arrived in the backpack. I hate to tell you this, Nick, but six of the nine scarlet macaws that came to the boathouse were dead."

Nick winced. Six out of nine? Two-thirds of them had died in the red backpack, drugged and taped up? How could anybody do that to a wild animal? As if—Nick remembered Mrs. F.'s words when she was talking about pets—as if scarlet macaws were as valuable as canned soda.

"When Carlos tried to back out of the deal, the smugglers threatened him," Nick's mother continued. "He had nobody to turn to for help. He hardly ever talked with the nuns. He knew they trusted him, wouldn't come near the boathouse, and had no idea what was going on. He was so desperate he threw one of the dead birds in the cow pasture when driving to town. He hoped somebody would realize something terrible was going on. When Peter's story appeared in the paper, the smugglers got tough."

"He sure was lucky they didn't do anything worse," Peter put in.

Nick's mother gave a grim nod.

"What'll happen to Carlos now?" Nick asked.

"The police aren't going to arrest him because he has agreed to be a witness against the smugglers. As for his job, it's up to the nuns if they want him to continue."

Wags was wagging again and prancing about, reminding them that it was way past her suppertime.

Peter said he had something for Nick and went with Nick and his mom to the police car. There, on the curb, was the deflated orange raft. The flippers and snorkeling equipment were safe and sound inside. The police had found them in a thicket behind the boathouse.

Nick grinned and put both thumbs up.

"We'll get together soon," Peter told Nick, "and we'll talk. I knew you could talk."

Nick looked up at his mother.

"Oh, he can talk," she said. "No question about that. Now if we can get him to take speech therapy, slow down, and make a good s, he could be on television. He could tell the world what happened today."

Nick punched her gently to tell her to shut up.

"I'm serious," she said. "You have a story to tell, Nick. An important story. I had no idea until today how much bird smuggling is going on in this country."

"You're right," Peter agreed. "Nick has an important story to tell. He can learn sign language, too, so deaf kids can hear it."

Nick's mother frowned at the mention of sign language.

Peter didn't notice, though. He turned to Nick. "You know, sign language could be useful under water."

Nick's eyebrows went up. Under water? Now

that was a neat idea. He glanced at his mother. She knew two languages. Why shouldn't he?

She gave a shrug.

Nick and Peter shook hands.

"How'd you ever meet him?" Nick's mother asked as the police car pulled away from the curb.

Nick grinned but said nothing. He felt bigger, more important.

"He's nice," she added. "Even though he's a sugar addict."

Nick leaned back, both arms around Wags. He didn't want to think about Peter, health food, and all that stuff. His mind had turned to the gray boat. Had the smugglers gone to the public beach or somewhere else farther down the lake? Would they hide the boat? Where should he start looking for the birds? Would he find more feathers?

14

Bright sunlight poured in through the window. Nick rolled over onto his other side to look at the clock. The digits read 9:30. He sat bolt upright. 9:30? He was turning into a bum! He had work to do!

Nick's mother opened the door and peeked in.

Wags squeezed through the door and came in, wagging her tail hard.

"Good morning, sweetheart," Nick's mother said.

Nick blinked. He hated being called sweetheart. And what was she doing at home at this hour?

She came in, closing the door behind her. "You're not going to run off to hunt for those birds right now, Nicholas Wilder."

Nick almost stuck his tongue out at her. Instead he asked, "How do you know that's what I plan to do?"

Her blue eyes looked calmly into his. "I knew last night when we were on the way home. Actually it was pretty obvious—I could see it in the look on your face."

"How?"

She gave a little shrug. "I guess you'd call it an intuition."

"A *what*?"

"An in-tu-i-tion. A kind of knowing."

"Do you hear this—this knowing—in your head?" He wanted to tell her how he'd heard Carlos's thoughts in his head and how he wouldn't have known what to do if he hadn't heard them. But he wasn't sure how to go about describing it.

She frowned and rubbed her chin. "I'm not sure I know what you mean. I'll have to think about it. But there's no question in my mind that you've found other ways to hear since you became deaf. You hear more with your eyes than most people hear with their ears."

She ruffled his hair before adding, "Someone is waiting for you in the kitchen."

"Who?"

"A man from New Haven. He wants to talk

with you."

"With *me*?"

"Yes. I told him he'd have to step over my dead body if he was going to wake you. You nearly fell asleep in your soup last night. You were really out."

"What does he want?"

"Answers to questions."

Nick made a face. "But I told the police *everything* yesterday." He looked around for his shorts and shirt.

Nick's mother handed him his hearing aid. "There are always more questions, Nick. You've got to be patient with people. Talk *is* pretty important. I bet some detectives get their intuitions when they're listening to people talking."

"He's a . . . ?" Nick didn't finish the sentence because he wasn't sure how to pronounce the word detective.

Nick's mother nodded. "He's a detective. And, by the way, the cops found the gray boat early this morning."

"Where?"

"In the woods at the east end of the lake."

"Did they find . . . ?"

She shook her head before he could finish the sentence. "They didn't find the birds, or the woman. But a man was picked up in New Haven. His picture was in the packet of photos Mrs. F. showed you last night."

Nick's mouth fell open. The cops had been working hard.

"I can't keep this guy waiting much longer. He's not an herbal tea drinker and I don't have any coffee in the house."

The detective was dressed in a gray suit and glossy silver necktie. He asked questions about the woman with the orange lipstick. Nick's mother helped Nick with his s words.

Then the man asked Nick to go with him to New Haven to see if he could identify the smuggler in a lineup. Carlos would be there, too.

"I'm coming," Nick's mother announced.

"What about the birds?" Nick asked the detective. "Where do you think they are?"

"Right now we're concentrating on tracking down the woman."

"But the birds might die . . . . "

"Our job is to find the woman. The parrots are probably with her."

"If they aren't . . . ?"

The officer shrugged and headed for the door.

Nick hands went into fists. Six scarlet macaws had died. Did the rest have to die too? He turned to look at his mother.

There was a fierce look in her blue eyes. Her lips moved silently without using any voice, "If they can't look for them, *we* will!"

Wags wasn't allowed in the New Haven police station. She had to stay in the car.

Nick saw Carlos before the gardener saw him. He looked bewildered as he stood in the waiting room beside a police officer from their hometown. Nick went right over to Carlos.

"B—!" Carlos gasped.

Nick couldn't get the words, but his mother understood. The gardener was overjoyed to see someone familiar. He'd thought he was going to be thrown in jail, even though he'd had a Spanish interpreter there to explain everything to him.

Carlos was taken to view the lineup. He was quite agitated when he returned. Nick was not allowed any time to communicate in any way with the gardener. The detective in the gray suit took him by the elbow and steered him down the hall.

Nick stepped into a dimly lit room with a large smoky window that looked out onto a stage. The air was thick and stale. As Nick moved toward the window, he realized his mother hadn't been invited in. He was alone with the cops. For a second he panicked. Would he be able to read their lips in the poor light? Would they be able to understand him? Would they believe him? Nick shivered as the door shut behind him.

Then Nick saw the six men standing in a row on the stage in the adjoining room. White cards with numbers hung from their necks. Their shoulders drooped and their expressions were grim.

For some strange reason, Nick's eyes were drawn immediately to number six, the last man on the left side of the stage. Even before he'd really looked at any of the suspects, Nick had the feeling number six was the man he'd seen the day before on the shore. The feeling scared him. In a flash he was remembering the doorknob turning this way and that while Carlos urged him to hurry and escape through the window.

Nick forced himself to examine number six. The guy was stocky, had dark hair, and wore glasses. Nick frowned. Glasses? He didn't remember any glasses. None of the men in the packet of photos Mrs. F. had shown him had worn glasses either. And this man wasn't wearing a mackintosh or boots.

Nick turned his attention to the other suspects. All were white. Two were short and thin—too short, too thin. The remaining three were fairly tall and heavyset, like the man with the glasses. One of them wore boots.

Nick squinted hard at the boots. As far as he could see, they weren't muddy. Had they been washed off in the lake?

The more Nick looked at the men, the more confused he became. He wished he'd looked more carefully at the man on the shore. What if he picked the wrong person? Would the smuggler go free? Or try to get back at Carlos?

Nick shut his eyes. What should he do?

One word kept echoing in the silence inside his head. *Six . . . Six . . . Six . . .*

Nick opened his eyes, took a deep breath, and pointed at number six.

The cops wanted him to say the number.

"Shh-ix," Nick stammered.

The detective cupped his hand behind one ear, urging Nick to speak up.

"Number SSS-IX!" Nick felt the *s* come out in a perfect stream and knew Mrs. Graves would have smiled.

The cops weren't satisfied, though.

A piece of paper and a crayon were thrust into Nick's hands. His face burned as he drew a large six. Did they think he was dumb—the way the woman with the orange lipstick had said he was dumb—and not worth bothering about? Darn them all! He could talk! He could, and he *would*!

Nick crumpled the paper into a ball. "It's number S S S-IX!" he said very, very slowly. He put six fingers up to be absolutely sure they understood. "I . . . ss-wear that's him!"

The detective patted Nick on the head and turned him around to let him know he could leave. A large slice of daylight shone into the room as the back door opened.

Nick's mother and Carlos weren't the only people waiting for him outside the lineup room. Mrs. F. and Peter were there, too.

"We've been chasing after you," Peter said

with a grin. He thrust a newspaper into Nick's hands. There, on the front page, was a photo of Nick with his mother and Wags. The headline beside it read, LOCAL BOY UNCOVERS SMUGGLING ACTIVITIES.

Nick wasn't allowed time to read it. Mrs. F. was tapping at him. "What happened in there?"

"There was a lineup. I picked this man with glasses. He..."

"Was it number six?" Nick's mother cut him short.

Nick nodded.

Peter and Mrs. F. exchanged a quick look. Nick saw the relief on their faces.

"Thank God you got him, Nick!" said Nick's mother. "I was sitting here saying the word six over and over and over."

"Mum," Nick whispered to her, "I think I heard you!"

She said nothing, but he saw the wonder in her eyes.

Carlos had figured out, from the expressions on their faces, that Nick had picked the right man. He stepped forward, took one of Nick's hands in both of his, and squeezed it gently, but firmly. There were tears in his eyes.

Nick nodded gravely at Carlos. Then he did something he never would have imagined doing. He threw both arms around the gardener and hugged him.

"Mum," Nick asked turning to his mother. "Will the nuns let Carlos shay?"

"We don't know yet."

Peter was tugging at Nick's arm. "I've got some really big news for you." He handed Nick a photo.

It was one of the photos from the packet Mrs. F. had shown Nick the day before. The guy in it was deeply tanned and was dressed in a snappy white Panama suit and hat.

Nick frowned and shrugged. He'd never seen the man before.

"It's him!" said Peter. "It's *him*!"

"Who?"

"The land developer."

What was Peter talking about?

"The man who wanted to buy the land across the lake."

Nick's mouth fell open. Their town had been swarming with bird smugglers!

"Where is he?" Nick asked.

"Gone," said Peter. "He cleared out fast. No one knows where he went. He just disappeared overnight."

"I bet he's with that woman," Nick's mother said. "Now, if I could get my hands on them . . . "

Mrs. F. waved to get everyone's attention. As Nick looked at her, he saw that she was dressed in jeans, an old purple sweatshirt, and black high-top sneakers. He clapped a hand over his mouth to keep from laughing. He'd never seen Mrs. F. in sneakers or jeans before.

The white bun on top of Mrs. F.'s head trembled as she spoke. "I'M ready to search ALL around the lake."

"For the birds?" Nick asked eagerly.

She jerked her head at him. "Of course? What else?"

Nick flushed. He'd thought he was the only person thinking about the missing macaws. "Do you think the smugglers drugged them?" he asked.

"We were talking with Carlos about that when you were in the other room," Nick's mother told him. "Carlos said the woman put gloves on, grabbed the birds, gave them some alcohol, and stuffed them in the backpack."

Nick grimaced. "All of them?"

Nick's mother, Peter, and Mrs. F. nodded.

"The police know about the backpack," Nick said. "Maybe the woman hid it in the woods."

"RIGHT!" Mrs. F. clapped her hands. "That's EXACTLY what I think. She wouldn't want to be caught with the scarlet macaws. That's all the proof the police would need that she's a smuggler."

"How long do you think the birds can survive in that backpack?" Peter asked.

Mrs. F. shrugged. "Depends what condition they're in. They survived it once. They might not be so lucky the second time—unless we get busy."

"Wait a minute," said Nick's mother. "If the woman hid the pack, maybe she intends to come back later to get it."

Nick shivered again. He hadn't thought of that possibility.

"Well, " Mrs. F. said firmly, "if she does, she's NOT going to find the macaws. WE are. Come on! Let's go!"

15

Two police officers joined the hunt for the scarlet macaws. When they all arrived at the public beach, they found the parking lot packed with people from town. Five of them wanted to help with the search. There were two fishers, another reporter, one of the guys from the Four Seasons Sport Shop, and Aaron Klein. Some of them had heard about Nick's adventure over the radio that morning. The rest had read Peter's story in the newspaper. The guy from the Four Seasons Sport Shop kept slapping Nick on the back as though they were old pals.

"You sure you want to come?" Nick asked Aaron.

Aaron nodded nervously and shoved his hands deep in his pockets.

"You can't chicken out when we're in the woods."

Aaron nodded again to show he understood.

"There might be snappers."

"I'll . . . I'll stay with you."

Nick shrugged.

To Nick's annoyance, Aaron really did stay with him. He followed Nick everywhere while plans for the search were being drawn up. He was like a burr stuck to Nick's back, just out of reach.

"He wants to be with you," Nick's mother said without voice when Nick complained to her. "He thinks you're a hero. Don't you like being a hero?"

Nick rolled his eyes and sighed. There were too many people around and he couldn't understand most of them. He wanted to go home, climb up high in the pine, and be quiet. It was strange how what had happened to him suddenly didn't belong to him anymore. But the birds *had* to be found. They would suffocate in the backpack. The more help they got for the search, the better.

Nick, Aaron, Carlos, Mrs. F., Wags, and Nick's mother were about to climb into the police boat for a ride to the east end of the lake, when Peter waved at them to stop. A nun had arrived. She wanted to have a word with Nick and his mother.

It was the same woman they'd seen at the police station the night before.

"This is the mother superior," Nick's mother told Nick.

Nick thought the nun looked awfully pale in her gray gown and white headdress, but her brown eyes were warm and friendly.

"So you're Nick Wilder?" she asked.

Nick nodded.

"I hear you're quite a swimmer. The lake's cold, isn't it?"

Nick nodded again.

"I came to thank you for what you've done for our convent."

Nick didn't know what to say so he nodded a third time.

Nick's mother gave him a "Speak up!" poke with her elbow.

"Uh—Mrs . . . " Nick's face got warm. How was he supposed to address her? "Uh . . . um . . . don't send Carlos away. . . . "

Her eyes were really smiling now. "We'll take care of him, Nick."

"You mean, he can stay?"

The mother superior nodded. "And I know he'll take care of us. He's the best gardener we've ever had."

The nun turned to Nick's mother for a few more words before they hurried to join the others in the boat. Nick's mother passed the good news on to Carlos.

They rode to the east end of the lake. Although the gray boat had been towed away, they could see where it had been hidden. There was a path that led through the woods to a dirt road. The smugglers had evidently used both the road and the path frequently because there were boot marks everywhere.

After two hours of searching both sides of the path and the dirt road and not finding anything—not even a snapper—the search team found themselves on the main road that led past the public beach to the turnpike. A police cruiser gave them a ride back to the public beach. Peter had tacked a map of the area up on a bulletin board at the beach and had gotten jugs of hot coffee and a mountain of donuts for the search teams.

"Any luck?" Peter asked Nick.

Nick and his mother shook their heads. Peter's face fell.

Mrs. F. didn't say anything. Her mouth was set in a grim line. Carlos sank down onto a bench.

Other teams returned one by one, empty handed.

Finally, at 1:30, they agreed to call off the search. All the helpers, except Aaron, left.

"We can't leave this junk on the tables," Nick's mother said.

"Junk?" Peter looked offended.

"It *is* junk," Nick's mother replied. "Those donuts are nothing but sugar."

Nick shut his eyes. Why'd his mother have to get going now? Peter wasn't trying to poison people.

"I'm sorry," Nick's mother said when he opened his eyes. "I'm pooped. And I'm worried about you and Carlos. How can I be sure you're going to be safe?"

"I don't think those smugglers will set foot in Connecticut again," said Peter.

He turned, dropped the coffee cups and left-over donuts into a couple of paper bags, handed them to Nick and Aaron, and nodded at the Dumpster at the end of the parking lot.

"It must've been scary yesterday," Aaron said as they walked the length of the parking lot.

Nick shrugged. He'd expected Aaron to complain during the search but he hadn't, not once.

"Weren't you scared?"

"I was cold," said Nick.

"You *weren't* scared?"

Nick was about to say yes, he had been scared, but Aaron's eyes were no longer on him. Aaron had stopped and was looking at the Dumpster with a strange expression on his face. Nick knew Aaron heard something.

What's that noise? Nick saw the thought in Aaron's puzzled eyes. *Is it a bird?*

In a flash, Nick had dropped his bag and was running. He ran past the cars and trucks. He ran right up the side of the rock beside the Dumpster, jumped down, and landed on the rusty metal lid. Foul smells stung Nick's nose and lungs as he strained to lift one of the two lids. It wavered in midair and then clattered open.

Nick peered down. There, half-buried in a heap of bottles, soiled Pampers, newspapers, and crumpled bags, was the red backpack.

Mrs. F. took the macaws out of the pack as carefully as a midwife delivering babies. The first one tried to bite her. She put it in Peter's car. The second one looked groggy. Mrs. F. laid it in Carlos's arms. The third one, bent double at the bottom of the pack, was clearly dead. Nick stroked the brilliant scarlet feathers as it lay on the grass.

"They're enormous!" Nick's mother said.

"*We* found them!" said Aaron. He couldn't stop grinning.

Mrs. F. wasn't ready to relax. "We've got to get them to the vet."

"How am I going to drive?" Peter asked.

The macaw perched on his steering wheel was squawking up a storm. Even Nick could hear the noise through his hearing aid.

"I'll get him," Mrs. F. said. She opened the door, grabbed the macaw quickly from the back, right near the eyes, and held it so it was unable to move its head. "HURRY!" she shouted.

Nick and Carlos hopped in the back of Peter's car with the other birds. Nick's mother followed in their station wagon with Aaron and Wags.

The receptionist's mouth dropped open when the search team came into the office with the macaws. They were ushered immediately into an examination room.

"Yup," Dr. Winter said, after examining the birds and putting the sick one in an incubator. "It looks like they were born in the wild." The metal bands on the birds' legs were from Mrs. F.'s store.

Everyone waited while the vet telephoned ornithologists at three different zoos around the country.

"Can they go back to the jungle?" Nick asked when Dr. Winter was through.

"I think they'd be better off in a zoo. The bird man at the Bridgeport Zoo is coming tomorrow to look at them. The birds will probably have to go into quarantine first, to be sure other animals won't catch any strange diseases from them."

Nick frowned. He wasn't too fond of zoos.

"It would be a long trip back to the jungle," Mrs. F. explained. "And there's the possibility they might be captured again."

"I wish I could keep them," said Nick. He remembered the chicken wire in the boathouse. "I could make my room into a cage. I could get all kinds of plants and branches."

Nick's mother made a face. "Not in *my* house."

147

Mrs. F. linked her arm in Nick's as they walked out to the parking lot.

"Will you work with me?" she asked.

"You mean . . . a . . . a job?"

"Yes. I think we're a pretty good team."

Nick looked from Mrs. F. to his mother. A job? A real everyday job?

"I'll pay you," Mrs. F. added. "In tropical fish, if not in cash."

"At the rate you're going," Nick's mother said, "you're going to be rich. Peter told me about the $20 he gave you. Maybe *I* should spend the summer by the lake while *you* work."

Nick punched her. "Mum, can I do it?"

She put a finger up. "Under one condition."

"What?"

"Guess."

Nick heard what she was thinking as he looked at her: *Take therapy. Show everyone you can do it.*

He rolled his eyes, but he didn't shut them. He gave one quick nod then he ran on ahead to join Wags in the car.

About the Author

Claire H. Blatchford lost her hearing overnight when she had the mumps at the age of six. She learned early on that there were other ways of hearing. She felt vibrations through her hands and feet, and heard the wind and the ocean through her eyes. And she learned that lipreading was about more than people's words, but also their expressions and gestures.

Ms. Blatchford attended regular schools and colleges, and in addition to her writing, currently teaches crafts at an elementary school. She and her husband have two daughters, a dog named Ginger, and two finches named Nut and Meg. They live in Connecticut.